OM.

Travelling Col

BRANCH LOCATED AT

NOSEHILL

THE QUEEN'S GRANT INHERITANCE

When young and beautiful nurse Anne Carter inherited her aunt's 300-acre estate and mansion, The Queen's Grant, it seemed the answer to a cherished dream. However, that dream would soon become a nightmare, with bitter enemies intent on parting her from her inheritance. Anne wondered which of the three attractive men who claimed to love her she could really trust, and she knew that her choice of life and love was certain to create a new path for her.

Books by Joanne Holden
in the Linford Romance Library:

HOLIDAY FOR A NURSE

JOANNE HOLDEN

THE QUEEN'S GRANT INHERITANCE

Complete and Unabridged

LINFORD
Leicester

Previously published in the
United States of America as
Nurse of Queen's Grant

First Linford Edition
published August 1993

British Library CIP Data

Joanne, Holden
    The queen's grant inheritance.—Large print ed.—
Linford romance library
I. Title II. Series
813.54 [F]

ISBN 0–7089–7413–9

Published by
F. A. Thorpe (Publishing) Ltd.
Anstey, Leicestershire

Set by Words & Graphics Ltd.
Anstey, Leicestershire
Printed and bound in Great Britain by
T. J. Press (Padstow) Ltd., Padstow, Cornwall

This book is printed on acid-free paper

1

"**A** FINE time to be getting butterflies in the stomach," Anne Rowe Carter told herself severely as she turned off the thruway and started on the last lap of her journey to Glenbrook, Massachusetts. "If I can stand the sight of an emergency amputation, I ought to be able to face problems at The Queen's Grant, even if I never owned more than a toothbrush before."

But the thought did nothing to quiet her nerves. As a registered nurse with three years' experience, Anne Carter knew about amputations and was trained to assist in surgery. She had had no experience being an heiress!

She saw the stop light just in time to step on the brake as a big truck roared across the intersection. That did it! She pulled up at the next lunch room and ordered black coffee while she tried to compose herself.

Sitting in the tiled and pungently mopped restaurant, Anne Carter felt more at home; it reminded her of the hospital cafeteria. She tried to marshal her thoughts. What was she afraid of?

Nothing, perhaps, except the unknown and, she admitted grudgingly, responsibility. Since her mother had died five years before, Anne Carter had been responsible only for herself. Now her mother's older sister, Mrs. Anne Rowe, for whom she was named, had willed her a three-hundred-acre estate — The Queen's Grant — a thirty-room house, completely furnished, and a couple named Mary and Jim Stone, who were the caretakers.

Her friends at the hospital had been openly envious of her good fortune.

"Boy," one nurse had whispered when they were both on night duty, "you've got it made. A honey-blonde with the face of an angel and the figure and lips of a temptress, green eyes and money in the bank! How will it feel to be a lady of leisure?"

"I'll never know," Anne Carter said honestly. "There's nothing I'd like less. And let me remind you, my aunt's estate — or any property that size — is bound to present problems."

"Problems like that I could take," another nurse said flippantly. "My problem is how to wangle a new evening dress out of an overloaded budget."

There was no use trying to anticipate the problems, Anne thought now. Aside from the lawyer's letter, there had been a stiff formal note from Mary Stone saying Anne Rowe's grandson, 'a very nice young man,' had come from Chicago and was staying in Glenbrook waiting to see her. Anne was not disturbed; obviously the man was an imposter!

Half an hour later, Anne Carter paid for her coffee and stepped out into the warm sunlight of a May afternoon. As she pulled on her driving gloves and

3

started the car on its last twenty-five miles to The Queen's Grant, she looked back on her years as a nurse, when she could manage her own life in her own way, as one of delightful freedom. Perhaps that was why she had refused so far to accept Dr. Steve's proposals.

There had been three proposals to date. Anne had not taken the first one seriously, but now Dr. Steve had developed a persistent streak, and each refusal only made him more ardent. If only he would give her time to think! It was true that Dr. Stephen Atkinson had a lot to offer; he was tall, dark-haired, with snapping black eyes. Anne had met him first almost a year ago when she was assisting in surgery at the hospital clinic. They had dated several times since.

She knew Steve was twenty-eight, that he had a well-established practice on Park Avenue; hospital rumor had it he was also independently wealthy. But to Anne his manner was too assured, too arrogant. In surgery, these qualities were an asset; in private life, they made him so demanding Anne had more than once protested:

'Steve, please! Don't tell me what to do or how to act as if you owned me! I'm over twenty-one, you know.'

But, Anne thought ruefully, it made no difference what she said. Steve had his own ideas, and he was so sure he was right it was impossible to argue. Only last night on the phone, he had tried to be dictatorial about her trip to Glenbrook.

"Just give the place to an agent and sell it off," he told her. "You don't have to drive all the way up there this weekend. We have a date Monday night, remember?"

"I'll be back," Anne promised. "I'm only staying overnight. But I've got to see it, Steve."

He had given a grudging assent, but his good night had been cool.

Anne shook off the recollection and gave her attention to the cloverleaf of the highway; finally she saw a sign: 'Glenbrook — 5 miles' and swung the car into the secondary road which ran past The Queen's Grant.

Anne was watching the mileage and automatically slowed as the needle neared the five-mile mark. Then she followed the curve — and there it was!

The Queen's Grant land sloped away from the road; the pillared façade of the house was mirrored in a large, serene pool in front of it. The place looked as if it had been transplanted from the South; the six white pillars were two stories high, topped by a third story with gable windows. Wings on either side balanced the house gracefully, almost as if it were a bird which had landed near the water. The hills rolling away in back of the house were suffused with the pale young green of birch and maple foliage and the darker green of pine on the slopes.

Anne Carter stopped the car and looked at her inheritance. As an unperceptive child nine years ago, she had seen The Queen's Grant only as the place where her aunt lived. Then she had been resentful because Aunt Anne wanted her and her mother to live there; the young girl had been jealous by being unwilling to give up even a small part of her mother's companionship. But as she looked at it today, the house had a personality of its own; Anne knew she could easily fall in love with it.

Abruptly she released the brake and started down the curving drive. She was almost at the columned porch when a small, towheaded boy in a red jersey and faded blue jeans darted out of the shrubbery and shot around to the door in the right-hand wing.

"She's here, Grandma!" he shouted shrilly. "You said she wouldn't come, but she did. She's here. Grandma, Grandpa! She's *here*."

The door opened suddenly, and the small figure was yanked inside without ceremony; then the door banged shut. Anne Carter drove on to the main entrance and got out of the car.

Well, she thought wryly, at least The Queen's Grant has its own herald. But it doesn't sound as if I were any too welcome.

* * *

Mary Stone was a small brown wren of a woman whose staccato gestures emphasized her nervous efforts to be welcoming. She wore a dark brown house-dress with a round white collar — evidently her version of a uniform — and her graying brown hair was pulled back neatly from a center part. Her eyes were brown, too, and almost completely round, giving her an expression of perpetual astonishment.

"Jim and me didn't think you'd bother to come way up here," Mary Stone said by way of greeting. "It's such a long drive and all. An since you're going to sell — "

"Who said I was selling?" Anne asked sharply.

8

"But of course a young girl like you wouldn't want to live here alone. Now, would you like a bite to eat? Or a cup of tea, maybe?"

"Thank you, no." Anne tried to repress the irritation she felt. "I stopped in a lunch room on my way up. I'll be here only overnight this time; I can't get away from the hospital for another week. But I'd like to have you show me around the house."

The door from the kitchen wing opened abruptly, and a big, lumbering man came in with the small boy. The child had been given a fresh jersey, this one blue, and a hasty swipe with a face cloth had momentarily given him a look of cleanliness which, Anne suspected, would be lost within the hour.

Jim Stone muttered something as his wife introduced him. Their grandson, Jim Martin, known as Butch, simply stared.

"Hello, Butch," Anne said cheerfully. "Thank you for announcing my arrival."

"Ain't you a nurse?" Jim demanded in an aggrieved tone. "Why ain't you dressed in white?"

Anne looked down at her fuchsia wool suit and smiled. "I wear a uniform only when I'm in the hospital," she explained.

But evidently Mary Stone gave a hidden signal; Butch was dragged off toward the kitchen again by his grandfather. Anne Carter looked inquiringly at the housekeeper, who said at once:

"We'll go around the rooms right now, if you want. The house is in three parts, like. This hall runs right from the front to the back, and the master bedroom is upstairs; Jim and me have our places over the kitchen wing."

Anne looked around the hall where they stood; it was wide enough to permit chairs and a desk of blond fruit wood on either side; the floor was paved with polished flagstones. The back door stood open, and she could glimpse the lush greenness of a conservatory. At her right, an archway showed a gracefully curving stair; the second floor balcony rail squared off the upper hall.

Taking a deep breath, Anne nodded to Mary Stone. "I'm ready for the grand tour. Let's go!"

As they went through the beautiful and graciously appointed rooms of the first floor, Anne became more and more impressed with the memories her aunt had left behind. She had stayed at Glenbrook only about a month each year, the housekeeper told Anne, but she liked to pick up souvenirs of her travels. Mrs. Rowe was constantly sending back furniture from France or Denmark, huge brass table-trays from Egypt, a samovar from Russia, an exquisite embroidered screen from China.

Anne remembered vaguely that her mother had once told her of her aunt's uncanny success with investments. She had pyramided a small legacy from her husband into a sound fortune. Anne's father, a professor of English, had been indifferent to money. When he died there was little left except a small insurance policy.

Anne had one bad moment when she entered the living room. It was large and sunlit; all pale yellow, white and chartreuse. Above the fireplace was a life-size portrait of her aunt sitting in a wicker chair in the garden, dressed in white lace; it had evidently been painted years earlier. Anne caught her breath; it was exactly as if her own mother were there, smiling gently at her.

"You'd better sit down a minute, Miss Carter," Mary Stone said, touching her arm. "That picture gives me a start sometimes, too. It's like she could speak. Ten thousand dollars she paid for it," the housekeeper added bitterly, "but a thousand was all she could spare for Jim and me, who took care of this place for nine years."

Anne Carter had less and less to

say as they went through a seemingly endless succession of rooms. The conservatory was like a tropical garden; the music room was a symphony in green and white with accents of coral; the library with its tall bookcases, the dining room with its exquisite Sheraton table and buffet, the breakfast room with its great bow window hung with hand-embroidered white lawn curtains — they were all too beautiful to be real. Anne could not even think about what she would do with the inheritance. It was too overwhelming.

Mary Stone had prepared her aunt's suite for Anne to use. The bedroom was huge, high-ceilinged, directly over the main entrance; the bed had a wrought-iron head rest and could, Anne thought, have slept three in comfort. In the sitting room, the muted colors of the oval Aubusson rug were repeated in the draperies, and an antique armoire with mirrored panels supplemented the two closets. They were rooms not for a mere princess, but for a queen!

Since she had said so little, at dinner Mary Stone apparently assumed Anne had merely been on a tour of inspection. She had set one place at the long mahogany table and lit candles; Anne wondered whether this was done to emphasize the loneliness of sitting at a great table with no one around.

"That grandson of Mrs. Rowe's — Robert — he's a very nice young man," the housekeeper said as she removed the consommé.

"Grandson!" Anne said sharply. "My aunt had only one child, a son, who died young, before I was born."

"Well, he looks like the family — blond and all," Mary said mildly. "Anyway, he's here in Glenbrook. He came from Chicago, and when he heard you might be here for the weekend, he took a room in town. I guess he ain't got the money to stay at the Park-Savoy; they say it costs a fortune. But I wouldn't ask him to stay here without your permission," said the housekeeper virtuously. "I sent him to a friend of mine in the village; I expect he'll be over tomorrow."

"I never heard of him," Anne repeated. "He must be an impostor."

"Oh, no!" Mary Stone said before she thought. She added lamely, "He's such a nice young man. He said something about taking care of his grandmother when she was sick."

"My aunt was staying at a hotel in Chicago when she had the heart attack," Anne said sharply. "She died in a hospital. Does this 'nice young man' intend to question the will?"

"I wouldn't know, I'm sure," Mary Stone said, suddenly cautious. "But when you sell — "

"Stop saying that!" Anne said irritably. "The Queen's Grant was left to me, and I'll live here if I want to."

After dinner Anne excused herself at once and went to the suite; she stretched out on the blue satin chaise longue in the sitting room. It was heavenly to close her eyes and stop thinking, at least for a minute.

But then her mind started going around in circles again. Mary Stone had said more than once she expected the estate would be sold, and had hinted broadly that she would be glad to help show the place, for a fee. As far as the housekeeper was concerned, Anne knew, she herself could go back to the hospital she had come from — and stay there!

The 'grandson' was an additional complication, who was probably counting on his nuisance value more than his credentials. Anne didn't intend to be taken in by him; she would tell him off in a hurry!

She finally roused herself and got ready for bed. Everyone, including Dr. Stephen Atkinson, took it for granted she would sell. Nobody asked her if she wanted to live at The Queen's Grant, Anne thought as she plumped the pillows resentfully. They simply assumed she had no mind of her own, no plans for the future, no interest in anything except a fat bank account.

She found a handkerchief and wiped away the angry tears.

The trouble was, Anne thought miserably, they were all so right. She could not live there alone!

2

THE dream was still with her when Anne awoke the next morning. She had fallen asleep thinking about the house, and in her dream she was going through the rooms again. But now they were no longer empty; they were filled with a succession of happy people all laughing and talking as they went through the beautiful place, as if they were in their own home. They were different in personality and in dress, but they all had one thing in common: they were gay and content; they were at home!

Sometime during the hours of sleep Anne Carter had found the answer to her problem. It had been there all along, she thought now as she stretched luxuriously and then slid out of bed. But it had taken her subconscious to spell it out for her.

She would make The Queen's Grant over into a rest home. For a brief six weeks when she was first capped, Anne had worked at a rest home about an hour's train ride from New York City.

The home had been planned as a research hospital, and the bare, austere corridors and uncurtained windows were still unchanged. Those who lived there sometimes stayed for only a short time. Others recognized it as 'the end of the line — the jumping-off place,' as one patient had told Anne. All were thoroughly depressed.

She had felt the same way about the institution and had found work in a hospital as soon as she could. But she had never forgotten the despair of those who, whatever the reason, had had to live in an antiseptic atmosphere and to look back, not forward.

With a mounting sense of excitement, Anne tried to think out her plan more carefully. She would establish a rest home that would be a model for the aged and temporarily homeless. She was not sure of the regulations, but she would find out. Meanwhile, she was suddenly free of carping criticism, from Steve, from a self-styled 'grandson,' from anyone. She knew what she wanted to do; her life would be worth-while!

The housekeeper eyed her uneasily when she came downstairs. "How do you like your eggs, Miss Carter?" she inquired. "I hope you slept well."

"Wonderfully well, thank you," Anne said cheerfully. "What a lovely morning! Just toast and jam, please, Mrs. Stone. Do you think your husband would have time to show me around outside sometime later?"

Jim would be available, the house-keeper told her. She served breakfast in silence but thawed somewhat when Anne complimented the blueberry jam.

"My own recipe," she said with the assurance of a competent cook. "Mrs. Rowe liked it real well. We have our blueberries — Oh dear!" she broke off.

"Our next door neighbor is here. Don't trust him, Miss Carter. I've heard he lays claim to the property."

"A grandson, and now a neighbor," Anne said with a shrug. "The more the merrier, I always say."

The man Mary Stone ushered into the breakfast room was tall and gangling. His face was not too homely, but his nose was large, and and his chin was definitely jutting.

"Mr. Bradford from next door," Mary Stone said briefly, and vanished.

Anne stood up. In spite of the housekeeper's attitude, this man was not ordinary. He carried himself with authority. Although his hair was an indeterminate color and his eyes a clear hazel, the force of his personality was immediately apparent.

"I'm Anne Carter," she said, holding out her hand. "And there's a fresh pot of coffee."

"Charles Hamilton Bradford Third," her guest said with a grin. "Brad to you. Coffee sounds wonderful."

They talked in generalities for a while, and then Charles Bradford came to the point.

"Our acreage adjoins yours," he said. "Roughly, your three hundred acres is a rectangle cut out of ours. When you sell, I'd like to bid on it."

"Who says I'm going to sell?" Anne demanded.

Bradford smiled. "Well, I just assumed — but let me talk for just a minute. Our land was a grant from Queen Anne, way back when."

"The Queen's Grant," Anne murmured.

"Yes, it was. But your aunt took over the name for her place. Frankly, my mother and father thought she was a shade presumptuous. After all, they didn't buy their acreage until 1834."

"Johnnie-come-latelys," Anne said, "in your opinion."

Suddenly Charles Bradford smiled, and Anne had to remind herself that this was the man Mrs. Stone had warned her against. Then he went on:

"It sounds ridiculous to us in this generation, but actually my father is distressed about a boundary dispute — involving only two acres, incidentally — and it seems easier to settle it this way."

"Your mother and father agree?" Anne asked.

"I haven't told them," Bradford admitted. "They're in Europe; Dad runs an export-import business; and I work with him. But I'm making this offer on my own. They would approve, I'm sure."

"Suppose I decide not to sell?"

Bradford looked at her blankly. "But what would you do with a place this size?" he asked.

"Oh, live here myself, maybe. Or turn it into a rest home, do something constructive . . . "

His expression was suddenly withdrawn; his face craggy. "It's your decision, of course," he said icily. If he had put it into so many words, Anne thought to herself, Charles Hamilton

Bradford Third could not have said more plainly:

'I don't believe you.'

He left soon afterward, and Mary Stone was obviously relieved. "Thinks he can get the place for a song," she muttered as she cleared the table. Anne decided to ignore the comment.

"Mrs. Stone, is there a doctor in Glenbrook?" she asked.

"I'll say!" the housekeeper said in surprise. "Of course Dr. Mark Hewitt seldom makes house calls any more, but I guess he's delivered almost everybody's baby for the last thirty years. Why?"

"I'd just like to meet him," Anne said noncommittally. "Is your husband ready to take me around outside?"

"He's ready, but right now you have another visitor, Miss Carter. It's the nice young man, your aunt's grandson."

"He hasn't convinced me of that yet," Anne retorted. "You run along, Mrs. Stone. I'll let him in."

Ready as she was to be cold to this stranger, Anne found herself taken aback by the appearance of the man at her door. He was about six feet three, with broad shoulders that stretched against his checkered sport jacket. His curly hair was only a shade darker than her own, and his eyes were pale gray; he was, Anne thought, the handsomest man she had ever seen. When he spoke, his voice was deep and resonant.

"I'm Robert Rowe. You're Miss Anne Carter?"

"Yes, I am."

"I'm sorry to come so early, but I was afraid you'd go back to New York before I had a chance to talk with you. May I come in?"

"Why, yes of course."

Feeling that the stranger, rather than herself had the situation well in hand, Anne walked ahead of him into the conservatory, where the morning sunlight made a dazzling display of the potted plants and hanging baskets. She sank onto the coral cushions of the wicker settee and indicated the chromium chair nearby. She decided to make the interview as brief as possible.

"As you mentioned, I have to go back to New York City today, Mr. Rowe. So you'll forgive me if I ask why you wanted to talk with me, and why no one has ever heard of my aunt's grandson before. You made no attempt to get in touch with my aunt while she was living . . . "

"Oh, but I did!" Robert Rowe said with a smile that softened the contradiction. "My grandmother had come to Chicago especially to see me when she suddenly passed away." At Anne's skeptical look, he added:

"Let me begin at the beginning, Miss Carter. You knew my grandmother had a son?"

"I knew my Aunt Anne had a son. But he died when he was very young. Somewhere in Mexico, I believe."

"He was my father," Robert Rowe said gently, "and he ran away from school when he was only eighteen. He met a girl in California; they eloped to Mexico. I like to think they had two years of complete happiness before my father was killed. After I was born, my mother came back to this country and lived with relatives in Chicago."

"And your mother never tried to get in touch with Aunt Anne?"

"No, but she left me a letter and gave me the name of the town in Mexico where they were married. My mother died several years ago."

"And the name of the town?"

Robert Rowe shook his head sadly. "It was wiped out in an earthquake some years ago. I have the marriage certificate, however, written in Spanish."

"Really?" said Anne. "You tell a touching story, Mr. Rowe, if that is your real name. But to me it lacks one essential quality — actual proof."

The housekeeper appeared suddenly in the doorway and flutteringly asked if Mr. Rowe would like a cup of coffee.

"No, thank you, Mrs. Stone," he

said as gratefully as if she had offered him champagne and caviar. "I don't want to keep Miss Carter talking on this glorious morning when she could be seeing the grounds."

"Tell your husband I'll be right with him," Anne said, angry with the housekeeper for assuming the role of hostess. The woman looked at her indignantly and withdrew.

"If you'll bear with me just a few moments longer," Robert Rowe said as if he were trying to be patient with a recalcitrant child, "I'd like you to come into the living room with me. You've seen the portrait of my grandmother?"

"I've seen the portrait of my aunt," Anne said haughtily.

"Did you notice the ring she is wearing?"

Anne looked at him, startled. "How did you know about the portrait?"

"Mrs. Stone was kind enough to show me around the house the day I came. She believes me, you see," Robert Rowe added.

"Whether the housekeeper believes you or not really makes no difference, does it?" Anne asked sweetly. "Aunt Anne left the estate to me."

"Tell me," Robert said as if he were making conversation, "how do you plan to sell the place? Furnished or — "

"I'm not going to sell. I've decided to make it into a rest home, a really beautiful rest home," Anne said firmly. It was Robert Rowe's turn to be startled.

"Someone as young and beautiful as you setting up a rest home! Oh, yes, you are a registered nurse, aren't you? Well, the idea does you credit, but I'm afraid I can't go along with it."

"That's all right with me," Anne said blithely. "You have nothing to say about it."

"Ah, but I have!" Robert's eyes were suddenly sharp.

"You're going to contest Aunt Anne's will?"

"I hope it won't be necessary," he said in a reasonable tone. "That's why

I came from Chicago — to talk things over. If we can arrive at an amicable settlement, out of court, we can save a great deal of time and money. You know sometimes this sort of litigation takes years. And there's always the danger that the major part of the estate will be awarded to the grandson rather than to a niece."

Anne was going to make a sharp retort and then thought better of it. He had a point. It would take time to prove he was an imposter, and meanwhile, it would be difficult to go ahead with her plans. Until she could think it over, it would be better to let Robert Rowe believe she was at least partly convinced.

"I have to go back to New York for a week," she said as if she might consider the idea of a settlement. "Why don't we wait until I come back?"

Robert Rowe smiled, and again Anne was struck with his charm. "Of course. But meanwhile, why not let me make myself useful? No matter what is done with the place, you should have an inventory of the furnishings; my grandmother was evidently quite a collector. I'm rather good at that sort of thing; I'm a furniture salesman. And I'd like to stay here, in the house. It will help speed things up, and I promise not to spirit away any valuables!" He grinned and added, "It would be a real act of kindness; that bed I have in the village is too narrow and too short."

In spite of herself, Anne could not repress a smile. Many beds would be narrow and too short for this young man. She did not like the idea of him staying in her house when she was not there, but it did seem ungracious not to let him have at least one of thirty rooms!

Anne glanced at her wrist watch and stood up abruptly. It was getting late; she would not have time for more than a casual look at the grounds. She would tell Mrs. Stone to expect him, Anne said, and she thought it would be useful to have the inventory made by someone competent.

Robert Rowe was on his feet instantly, and he was so pleased with himself Anne wondered if she should have extended the invitation after all. But he gave her no chance to back out.

"Well, I certainly do thank you, Miss Anne Carter," he said with sincerity. "And now, if I can impose a few seconds more, could we go and look at the portrait?"

"Can't it wait until I come back?" Anne protested.

"It will take only a second." He let her precede him down the hall to where the double doors of the living room stood open. Reluctantly, Anne went and stood before the portrait. Aunt Anne had been fifteen years older than her mother, but the picture had been painted several years before, and the resemblance to Anne's mother as she was just before she died was uncanny.

"Look at the ring on my grandmother's left hand," Robert Rowe urged.

It was a large oval stone surrounded by diamonds, and Anne thought it must have been very beautiful.

"What is the center stone?" she asked. "I can't quite see the color. Is it an amethyst?"

"No, it's smoky topaz," her visitor said. "My grandmother bought the stone on a trip to India and had the ring made up in her own design."

"Oh?" For the first time since she had met him, Anne felt a chill of premonition. "How do you know?" she demanded.

"Because Grandmother gave it to me when she was out in Chicago, before she passed away." He took a small box out of his jacket pocket and pressed the clasp. The ring in the picture seemed to be exactly the same as the one the box revealed.

"You see," Robert Rowe said huskily, "Grandmother believed me. I think you will come to believe me, too."

3

"MY cousin Betts' engagement party is sure to be a smash," Dr. Stephen Atkinson told Anne when he called for her that evening.

Instead of using his own car, he had hired a limousine with a chauffeur for what he called their evening on the town. As he settled beside her on the luxurious seat, he said, smiling, "We've got to act like the other guests — look like a million, you know. As you do, Anne. That's a nice dress," he added in what would have seemed an understatement from nearly any other man but was, Anne knew, the wildest kind of flattery from Steve Atkinson. He let himself grow lyrical only when describing a particularly intricate operation, she had noticed.

The nice dress had cost Anne almost

two weeks' salary and at that was only a reproduction of a Paris model which, the saleslady had assured her, had cost the film star for whom it was made more than a thousand dollars.

"I think it's nice, too," Anne said demurely.

"And I like that little shoulder thing that goes with it," Steve went on.

The 'little shoulder thing' was known in high fashion circles as a demi-topper, a shawl-like wrap of the same lilac brocade as the dress. Anne smiled her appreciation of Steve's compliment.

"I see it's high in front," Steve went on, evidently determined to go all out in his approval. "I like that."

Wait till he sees the back, Anne said to herself. The bodice, fitted in front, was slashed to the waist in back, giving a general glimpse of her smooth white skin. There was a pert bow to indicate the end of the décolletage.

Her reckless expenditure for the outfit was more than justified, Anne felt, when the limousine drew up before the night club entrance where cousin Betts' engagement party was to be held. Her family had taken over the whole place for the event.

"I feel like a movie star," Anne giggled in Steve's ear as he helped her out of the car. The sidewalk was a solid mass of people of all ages, held back from a cleared space by ropes stretched from the curb to the doorway. Policemen stood by, and dinner-jacketed attendants — connected with the hotel where the night club was located — were bowing to arrivals. Farther along, in the lobby, cameras were being aimed as notables stood smiling, their jewels outflashing the flashbulbs, where they were photographed for newspapers and magazines.

Steve took Anne's arm and steered her through the crush and into the night club itself. There cousin Betts and her fiancé stood with their parents near the entrance to the big room. It was all green and gold, repeating the color of Betts' gold lamé dress with its cluster of green orchids on one shoulder.

They paused for a moment while Steve introduced Anne to the group; everybody murmured polite phrases, but most of the words were lost in the general cacophony of voices.

There was a table with Steve's name on it, a small one just for two, in a corner near a green-cushioned banquette. They were barely seated when with a roll of drums from the band, the lights were suddenly dimmed and candles were lit on every table. At the same time a flower-garlanded sign on the wall became visible, with the names of the engaged couple shining in luminous paint. It looked like a treasured manuscript from the Middle Ages.

Music from recent hit shows rippled in the background; waiters moved expertly among the tables; some of the young irrepressibles were already having a great time dancing their individual versions of the latest dances or — Anne suspected — inventing dances of their own. The orchestra also played danceable tunes calling for the traditional 'touch' dancing, and at the first note of such a number Steve drew Anne out onto the dance floor.

"I can't compete with these young acrobats, Anne," he said. "This kind of dancing is for me, where you get to hold a girl in your arms instead of circling around her, or vice-versa, or bending double so that your cranium all but bumps the floor!"

Anne tucked her head under his chin. "Touch dancing suits me," she murmured. "I never had a yen to be a circus performer, either."

Between dances and watching the table-hoppers — everybody seemed to know everyone else — and nibbling at the various supper dishes, they managed only the most fragmentary talk. Then Steve said suddenly:

"Look at me, Anne."

Anne obeyed. "You're special, Steve. Is that what you wanted me to notice?"

"No, I just want your undivided attention. I want to talk with you seriously."

"Here?" Anne's eyes widened in astonishment.

"The best place," said Steve. "The atmosphere, the flowers, the music — just the background for what I want to say. An engagement party is romantic. Couldn't it be our engagement party, too, Anne?"

"But, Steve — "

"I know; you're thinking of Glenbrook. You think you've been fingered for a Dr. Schweitzer role because your aunt left you that place in the wilds of Massachusetts. You want to dedicate your life to helping humanity on a grand scale. But why should you bury yourself in the hills? Look at all the fun we can have together, here in New York. Aren't you happy now? You're so young and lovely."

"Thank you," Anne said softly as Steve paused for breath.

At that moment a young man Steve

had introduced to her earlier came over to their table, held out his hand to Anne without a word and looked questioningly at Steve. Anne, in turn, looked at the now scowling Dr. Atkinson.

"Oh, go on! Dance with him," said Steve ungraciously.

The young man, whose name turned out to be Frederic Van Hyssen, whirled her deftly into the infinitesimal space that opened up among the gyrating couples. Then, for the first time, he spoke.

"Possessive, isn't he?" he commented. "Engaged?"

"No."

"Wants to be, though," observed the taciturn Mr. Van Hyssen, and lapsed into silence again for the remainder of the dance.

Flushed and breathless and laughing, Anne was returned to her table. Steve got up and bowed, unsmilingly; Frederic also bowed and went off, patting Anne's arm by way of farewell.

"Never liked that guy," Steve observed, when they had started on the delectable salmon tart the waiter brought. "He was in medical school with me. Dropped out. Course too much for him; he hadn't the necessary gray cells. Went into advertising, I heard."

Anne did not reply. She knew this mood of Steve's — belligerent, ready to find fault with anyone or anything.

Oh, dear, she thought, he's furious because of my Glenbrook project. He wants me to give it up, to stop thinking about it, even. But I can't give it up; I won't! She tried to lead the conversation into safe channels.

"Your cousin Betts and her fiancé make a stunning couple, don't they?" she said brightly.

"Betts and Lou? Oh, yes. They're both good-looking. Too good-looking. Their marriage won't last."

"Just because they're both handsome?" Anne was bewildered.

"That, and because they're vain and

41

a couple of spoiled brats. Too much of the same background. No surprises in a combination like that."

"Then you think only people who come from different backgrounds can be happy together?" asked Anne, feeling that she had directed their talk away from a possible harangue against her Glenbrook project. But a moment later Steve returned to it.

"You'd never make a go of that rest home stuff," he said abruptly. "You've had no business experience; you're young and helpless. Besides, this grandson — imposter or not — could be a real problem."

"I don't worry about him! And I'm a trained nurse," Anne reminded Steve sharply. "Twenty-two is not exactly infantile."

"What you should do," Steve went on as if she had not spoken, "is sell the place. You'll need to get a good agent to do that. Then put the money aside for a nest egg; a married woman should have some money of her own."

"But I'm not — " Anne began.

"There! That's civilised music they're playing now. We'd better take advantage — "

It was going to be awfully hard to get Steve to see her side of the rest home idea, Anne reflected as she followed her partner's lead around the room. The floor was more crowded than ever, and Anne was rocked back on her heels as another man bumped Steve.

"Sorry," said Frederic Van Hyssen.

Steve merely scowled by way of acknowledgement. To Anne he muttered: "People who fall over their own feet ought to keep off the floor."

They got into step again — Steve was a good dancer — and for a while he guided Anne smoothly through the throng. Suddenly he was bumped again, this time harder than before. He stood stock-still and glared at Frederic Van Hyssen, again at fault.

"What's the idea?" he demanded. "If you want to mix it up, we can step into the corridor."

"Gee, Steve, old boy, I'm sure enough a clumsy oaf," said Van Hyssen with a deprecating smile. Suddenly Steve and Anne, standing still with his arm around her, were bumped from another direction with considerable force.

"Move, fella!" shouted the offender, and danced by with his partner. Steve led Anne back to their table as Van Hyssen and his girl disappeared in the crowd.

"That's what comes of encouraging a boor like that," Steve said, his accusing eyes on Anne's face.

"But I didn't!" she protested.

"You looked mighty chummy when you were dancing with him," he retorted. "If Fred comes over here again, I'll punch him in the nose."

"Oh, Steve," sighed Anne, "can't we forget him?"

Steve was silent for a moment and then he smiled shamefacedly. "You're right. I'm acting like a boor myself. But I'm on edge, Anne. When you

44

talk about embarking on a wildcat scheme that will bring you nothing but discouragement, I — "

"You can't say that! You haven't seen the place, and I have. It's a beautiful house and a stunning view — miles and miles of green hills off into the distance — "

"Anne, listen to me. I say sell the place and save yourself the headaches."

"Shhh!" came sharply from a table nearby.

"If you think it over, really think — " Steve continued in a lower tone. He hadn't noticed that a girl in a white dress, sparkling with crystal beads that blazed in the spotlight, was standing on the dais with the band. She had a microphone in her hand and had already begun to sing.

Now a whole chorus of 'sh-h-hs' rose around them, and Steve subsided. He leaned back in his chair and made no effort to conceal his boredom as he watched the singer. When she finished amid deafening applause, he started to talk to Anne again. But the singer, after a few bows, returned to the mike and smilingly began another song. This was repeated for a third time, and Anne felt sorry for her escort. She reached over and patted his hand where it lay on the table.

The singer's third song finally concluded, and Steve brightened. But his ordeal was not yet over. The young singer suggested everyone join her in the lively 'Today is Monday!' The crowd started slowly but came in strong on "Today is Tuesday!" By the time they came to "Today is Wednesday," they were on their feet to shout the chorus: "Everybody happy? Well, well, well, I should smile!" They sat down again, but the infectious tune called for another round, Monday through Sunday. The guests applauded themselves, as well as the singer, as the song came to an end.

"At least it's over," said Steve, but he spoke under his breath. Those around him were laughing and enjoying themselves immensely; he didn't want to incur further disapproval. He returned to their private conversation.

"I don't believe it will be safe for you, living up there in the mountains, especially since you have invited the 'imposter' to move in."

"I didn't ask him to stay indefinitely; not while I'm not there. And there is a married couple, the caretakers," Anne protested. "I'll add a staff later; it's a big place."

"It would be different if you married me and we were doing the job together," Steve persisted. "But I couldn't consider leaving my practice here in New York. You wouldn't ask that?" He looked at Anne questioningly, but she knew he wasn't really asking. She was supposed to say no. She said it.

"The house is probably a firetrap," Steve went on gloomily. "A small town like Glenbrook can't have an adequate fire department. Even if you had a good water supply, it would be dangerous . . . How *is* the water situation, by the way? Have you looked into it?"

"Not yet," said Anne, determinedly cheerful. "But I stayed overnight, and the water in the bathroom came from a faucet. I didn't have to drag it in from the well in a pail."

"It's not a laughing matter," said Steve severely. "Your carelessness about details when you plan to take on something like this proves that you need someone to look after you. You know I want to marry you, Anne."

"I guessed it," Anne said, dimpling. "You've said something like that every time we've had a date for the last three months."

"I wasn't talking off the top of my hat! I wangled the invitation for you to this engagement party because I thought an occasion like this would put you in the right mood.

"It hasn't worked out quite that way," Steve said with a wry grin, "but I'm a persistent guy." He took a velvet box out of his pocket and pressed the clasp. "My love goes with this," he said huskily, pushing the box across the table.

She gasped at the square-cut emerald, shooting fire as if defying her to refuse it. "An emerald!" she breathed. "The most beautiful thing I've ever seen. Oh, Steve! I can't take it. With this ring you're not only asking me to marry you — but more."

"Marriage is more."

"Please try to understand, Steve. If you really love me, try to see my point of view. I want to do something worth-while in the world, Steve. I have a dream, and I want to make it come true. If you see things the way I do, I can take this ring. If you don't, we have a long way to go."

"But you're crazy," Steve protested.

Anne put the ring back in the box and pressed it into his hand. "Think about it, Steve. I like you; maybe I love you. But before I promise to be true to you, I have to be true to myself."

There was a sudden silence throughout the room as if everyone was breathless. Then there was a concerted "Oh!"

"Man going to jump off the roof!" someone shouted. "He's up there on the ledge."

Dr. Steve Atkinson instantly got to his feet and pulled Anne up with him.

"One side, please," he said with authority. "I'm a doctor and this is a nurse. Let us pass." The crowd parted respectfully.

Towed along by his firm hand, Anne found herself in the elevator, shooting upward to the roof. Two policemen met them as they emerged into the warm night. Steve spoke to them in a low voice and then turned to Anne.

"No one dares to come too close for fear it will trigger the jump," he said. "They're spreading a net on the sidewalk, and someone is speaking to him from the window directly below the ledge. I think we'd better go down there, too. Maybe if I talk to him, casually, about Cousin Betts' engagement party, it will take his mind off his own problems long enough to let a policeman sneak up here on the roof."

The night which had seemed warm to Anne when they first emerged on the roof, was suddenly chilly. She shivered as she followed Steve to the room below the dangling legs of the man sitting on the ledge, eighteen stories above the street.

4

ANNE never did get to see the face of the man who had threatened to jump. In a surprise move, she found out later, the police had managed to get a rope around him from above, and he was pulled onto the roof and safety. Anne looked down at the street to where the firemen were still holding the net, evidently to make sure the man did not break away from his captors. She shuddered at the height and said to Steve:

"I get dizzy only looking down; I wonder the poor man didn't fall off the ledge. He must be desperately unhappy."

Dr. Steve Atkinson shrugged. "That type never knows whether he's unhappy or not. He likes to be the center of attention, that's all. And he won't stop with this one try. He'll keep at it again and again until he finally *does* succeed."

It was a doctor's way of looking at attempted suicides, she knew, but Anne still felt there must be something someone could do. As they waited for the elevator, she said impulsively to Steve:

"Would your cousin Betts mind terribly if we left her party early? I don't believe I can get back in to a party mood."

"Cousin Betts won't mind," Steve said at once. "In fact, she probably won't even miss us. And frankly, with my operating schedule tomorrow, I'll welcome the chance to get a little extra rest."

In the limousine going home, Anne told Steve how much she had enjoyed the engagement party, and tried again to present her point of view on making The Queen's Grant into a rest home. Steve answered only in monosyllables, so she finally gave up. They were

53

almost at her door before he said:

"I understand you're taking a leave of absence starting this weekend. But don't think you've seen the last of me, Anne Rowe Carter; I'm the persistent type. No matter where you go, I'll follow you, and I'll keep asking you to marry me until you say 'yes.'"

"Of course I want you to come up and see The Queen's Grant, Steve!" Anne said warmly. "Then I think you'll understand why I've fallen in love with the place."

"In love with the place but not with me!" Steve said bitterly.

"Steve, I'm half in love with you, really. But I can't accept such a gorgeous emerald until I'm sure. I must be honest with myself as well as with you."

"I thought you'd rather have an emerald than a diamond because it matches your eyes," he said as if he had not been listening.

"It's beautful, perfectly beautiful," Anne said.

During the next few days, Anne was so busy she scarcely had time to think. She packed her trunk and sent it on ahead first thing, but she did splurge on a set of matched luggage to take with her in the car and unfortunately passed a table of new swim suits as she was going out of the store, and succumbed to a strapless green satin that fitted so perfectly it might have been designed for her. Luckily she was working the three to eleven shift, but even so she had to run a little to get back to the hospital on time.

But Anne forgot about her weariness on Saturday morning when she was finally in the car and crossing the line into Connecticut. She was starting her great adventure. She would prove herself. From now on, nothing and no one would stop her!

Later when she whirled the car down the drive and stopped before the front door, she sat for a moment just looking at it. The house was even better then she remembered; the sun glinted on the multi-paned windows, and the brass fittings of the big front door gleamed as if in welcome.

"It's an inviting house," Anne whispered to herself as she got out of the car. The big door opened as if in response to the words she could hardly hear herself.

"Hi there! You must have made good time. Mrs. Stone and I were giving you another hour."

Robert Rowe stood in the doorway, dressed in an electric blue pullover and white walking shorts. He was as handsome and charming as ever, but to Anne's mind his manner had taken on a new assurance, as if he were the owner, welcoming a guest.

Without waiting for an answer, he came out to the drive and said cheerfully: "Your trunk came. It's upstairs in your room. Let me help with your luggage . . . "

"It's in the back," Anne said shortly.

"I'd like to go right upstairs."

"Of course," he agreed. "Our hotel service is perfect here. The bellboy — that's me — will take you to your room, and then I'll come down and put your car away while you freshen up. When you're ready, Mrs. Stone has prepared a sort of high tea that has me drooling with anticipation. I suggested she set up the table in the English garden so we can enjoy the view and the sunshine."

"How thoughtful you are," Anne said sarcastically as she followed Robert Rowe into the hall and up the curving staircase. "I see you've managed to acquire a nice tan in spite of your labors indoors — taking inventory, I mean."

"Taking inventory is quite a job," he said cheerfully. "It will take some time, so I thought I'd enjoy the good weather; I can catalogue even after dark. By the way, do you mind if I call you Anne? And call me Bob, of course. We are related, you know."

Anne was going to dispute the statement, but then she shrugged. There would be time for argument later. "It's all right with me," she said indifferently. Without thinking, Anne stopped in front of the door to the suite she had stayed in before. But Bob was proceeding nonchalantly along the hall.

"Hold it, Bob!" she commanded. "This is the suite I slept in last time."

"Yes, I know. Mrs. Stone told me," Bob said calmly. "But it has the biggest bed in the house, and we thought you wouldn't mind the room in the east wing. It has its own balcony, overlooking the English garden and the lily pool, with a backdrop of dwarf cedars. Reminds me of a garden I saw in Cornwall when I was in England last year — as you remind me of the perfect type of English beauty. I've put the chaise longue in there, and your trunk, of course."

Bob continued resolutely down the hall, and Anne marched after him, so angry she could scarcely think. He opened the door at the end of the hall and stood aside, holding her luggage. When she went in, Anne remembered seeing the room before and had to admit it was charming. It was a long room, with the bed set against the far wall and the French windows open onto the balcony with its wrought-iron rail. The wallpaper was patterned in gray pussy willows with only a faint hint of pink here and there, and Bob had been thoughtful enough to put a bowl of pink roses on the dressing table.

He opened the closet door and put the luggage inside before he turned around and looked at her closely.

"Your trunk is in there, too," he explained. "It's a very large closet. But of course if you don't like this room — "

Anne walked out onto the balcony and looked down on the garden and lily pool below. A table for two was already set, and Mrs. Stone came out of the kitchen carrying a silver tea service. She knew Bob had crossed the room and was standing in the opened window space.

"I like all the rooms in this house," she said without turning around, "but I think it was mighty high-handed of you to take the master suite without consulting me."

"You weren't here, Anne . . . "

"There are methods of communication," she reminded him icily, "and I don't mean the pony express. We have a telephone service at the hospital twenty-four hours a day."

"I'm sorry," Bob Rowe said, sounding truly contrite. "I'll move my things out first thing in the morning . . . "

"No — let it go," Anne said wearily. "There are more important things to discuss than the question of rooms. Stay where you are for the time being."

Mary Stone, hearing their voices, looked up and gave a little bobbing nod as Anne spoke to her. "I'll be down in a few minutes," she said.

Turning quickly, she surprised Bob with his hand upraised in salute to the housekeeper.

There was no doubt about it, Anne thought as she brushed her hair vigorously after Bob had gone, Mary Stone was completely won by the 'grandson' and he, in turn, was playing up to her. She had not seen Bob's complete gesture, but Anne had no doubt it was one of elation, indicating Anne had agreed to the switch in rooms.

★ ★ ★

Dr. Mark Hewitt was short and rotund, with a thatch of silver-white hair and a rosy complexion. Yet he had little of the jollity usually associated with a man of his appearance and years. In fact, as Anne Carter introduced herself in the old-fashioned office of his home in Glenbrook, his manner was entirely professional.

"You're a nurse, eh? Is this a

courtesy call? I take it you are in perfect health."

Anne smiled. "Yes, I feel fine. But I do need advice."

Dr. Hewitt looked at her sharply, but his manner softened. "Sit down, my dear. It has been my experience that most people who seek advice are asking only to be told they are right." As the quick color rose in Anne's cheeks, he chuckled. "Never mind; I'm here to help. What do you want to ask me about?"

Although he had been delivering babies for many years, probably he had not been in Glenbrook when her aunt had a child, Anne began. But perhaps he might have some information about the boy. Dr. Hewitt shook his head.

When he had taken up practice in Glenbrook, he explained, Anne Rowe's boy was already in school. Later on, he had heard he had run away to Mexico. He had never treated Mrs. Rowe, he added, although he had met her several times. His information about the boy and his death as a young man had been more or less gossip. After the boy died, Mrs. Rowe had been in Glenbrook only at intervals, and she had never consulted him.

"Did you ever hear of Aunt Anne's son getting married?"

The doctor chuckled. "I gather you don't believe in this 'grandson' who has turned up. I hear all the gossip, my dear. But frankly, I don't know. It's possible he has a legal claim, and in that case it is a legal problem; not one for a poor old country doctor."

"Yes, it does concern you," Anne said with spirit. "Bob Rowe wants me to sell the place and give him part of the money. I don't want to sell The Queen's Grant."

"You don't want to sell! Are you going to live there all by yourself? Oh, no. Of course you'll get married — "

"I want to make the estate into a rest home," Anne said abruptly. "Not an institution; a home, a place where people will enjoy living. Please help

63

me, Dr. Hewitt. Everyone has been so discouraging."

She had the doctor's keen attention now, although he took a cigar out of his desk drawer and lighted it before he spoke. Then his voice was gruff and he had to clear his throat.

"I've had a dream for many years, but somehow I never thought a beautiful blonde nurse would know about it, or even think of making it come true. But let's be practical. You know the need is great. Older people who are healthy and moderately active, like myself," he said with a grin, "find it increasingly hard, if not impossible, to maintain establishments of their own. Yet the alternative — living with their children or other relatives — often isn't feasible and is usually uninviting."

Anne Carter was suddenly at ease. She had found an ally in Dr. Hewitt. They spoke the same language and they had the same dream. For the better part of an hour, however, Dr. Hewitt pointed out the problems which would be involved in carrying out her plan. There were regulations as to fire precautions, wiring and even the floor space allotted each guest. There might be a certain amount of rebuilding that would have to be done.

"Yes, I know," Anne agreed, "but these details can all be ironed out as I go along. If you'll help me, Dr. Hewitt, I don't mind the problems. And who knows? — if we make a success of The Queen's Grant, others will follow our example. But I must have someone on my side."

Dr. Hewitt looked at her shrewdly. "I gather your young man isn't on your side," he said flatly. "Is he a doctor?"

Steve was a doctor, but he was not her young man, Anne retorted. She explained as best she could her relationship with Dr. Atkinson, and Dr. Hewitt nodded without comment. Then he returned to the problem of the grandson.

"I'm sure he's an imposter," Anne said firmly, "but I haven't figured out what to do about it. There's also another problem: Brad — Charles Hamilton Bradford Third — wants to buy the place. To settle a boundary dispute, he says."

Again the doctor nodded. "Yes, that's what I heard."

"So," Anne said ruefully, "maybe I'm asking you to fight a lost cause. Perhaps you don't want to be a supporter of defeated forces."

Dr. Hewitt leaned back in his chair and blew a smoke ring.

"You don't know me very well, Anne Carter," he said, smiling. "I've been tilting at windmills all my life. There were times, when I delivered a premature baby or treated a man who had been chewed up by a tractor, when I thought I couldn't win. But it was worth a try. If you want to set up a rest home at The Queen's Grant, I'm with you all the way. Now let's get down to brass tacks."

When she left Dr. Hewitt some time later, Anne was elated. He was going to get in touch with the Public Health Service of the state and get a copy of the regulations; he would make sure they had all the facts before they proceeded.

Yet when Anne left it was not his offer of help that remained with her but Dr. Hewitt's staunch belief in her idea and the wonderful knowledge she had found a friend.

She drove back to The Queen's Grant in high spirits, to be met by Mary Stone, who was standing on the front steps.

"You don't have Butch with you?" she asked distractedly. "I told Jim you didn't. That boy will be the death of me yet."

"Mrs. Stone, why are you taking care of Butch?" Anne asked. "Is his mother sick?"

"No, she works," Mary Stone said shortly as if, Anne thought, Butch's mother were engaged in a nefarious trade.

At that moment a bedraggled figure

came around the corner; Butch was so thoroughly plastered with mud his hair was no longer blond.

"I fell in the brook," he explained briefly. But that was as much as Anne heard about the mishap. Mary Stone whisked her grandson inside and, from the subsequent yells, Anne gathered Butch was being either washed or punished.

Probably the same thing for him, Anne told herself as she drove the car around in back and put it away.

5

BOB ROWE, as devious as Anne thought him to be, was still a model house guest, she reflected a few days later. He was never obtrusive, and although he was usually in the house for dinner, he busied himself with projects around the estate and so endeared himself to Jim Stone as well as to his wife. More than once Anne wondered if she were not the one in the wrong. Perhaps it would be best if she compromised with Bob, with Brad, and with her own convictions.

But this she could not do. She had been trained to think of others, and there were many who needed her help. How could she sleep nights if she failed to set up a rest home, although limited as to the number she could take in? She could at least establish a model for helping others to live graciously and comfortably!

"Man does not live by bread alone, you know," she told Butch as she wandered out into the English garden after breakfast. The small boy, his face already smudged, looked at her blankly.

"Did Indians eat bread?" he demanded.

"I believe they ate a bread made of corn meal," Anne said, unsure of herself on this point. "Are you interested in what the Indians ate, Butch?"

"I guess maybe they ate deers and rabbits and stuff mostly," Butch said. "They used to shoot them with bows and arrows, y'know. Grandpa says there's Indian arrowheads all around this place, if I can find them."

"Your grandfather is right, I'm sure," Anne agreed.

"I wish I'd been born an Indian," Butch said disconsolately. "Then I could have my own bow and arrow and shoot deers maybe."

"You wouldn't want to shoot a deer, fella," a masculine voice said pleasantly. Charles Hamilton Bradford came into

70

the garden with an apologetic grin for Anne. "Mrs. Stone told me you were out here."

"I would so shoot a deer," Butch contradicted, but he left the discussion at that and vanished in the direction of the woods.

"You know, Miss Carter," Brad said, shoving his hands into the pockets of his slacks in an embarrassed gesture, "I rather got off on the wrong foot when I first met you, talking about old boundary disputes and all. I wonder — can't we start over? We *are* neighbors, and whether you sell The Queen's Grant or keep it, there's no reason we can't be friends."

Anne looked at him, wondering if there was some ulterior motive behind his offer of a truce. But his gaze was candid and his voice sounded sincere. She smiled and said:

"Neighbors *and* friends. That's the way I'd like it."

"Then may I welcome you to Glenbrook?" Brad said, smiling in

71

turn. "If you would honor me, I'd like you to be my guest at a dinner party at the Park-Savoy, say next Saturday?"

"Why, that's lovely of you!" Anne exclaimed. "I don't know anyone here except Dr. Hewitt; I talked with him about making this a rest home."

"We'll include Dr. Hewitt then; he's a fine old gentleman," Brad said graciously. "Cynthia Boynton, a friend of mine from St. Louis, is staying at the hotel for a few weeks; I'll ask her. And perhaps Bob Rowe should be invited, too?"

Anne agreed, although with mental reservations. Perhaps later she could discuss Bob's claim to the estate, but she was wary of Brad's sudden overture of friendship. Still, she felt obligated to make some gesture in return.

"About the two acres you mentioned that were involved in the boundary dispute," she began, "how did it all start?"

"If you like, we can walk over to the place where the markers are and I'll show you." Brad offered. "It may be rather rough going, but you have low heeled shoes, and it isn't too far."

Anne was enthusiastic about the idea and said so. They walked down the path toward the woods, past the horn which had been converted into a garage and to a point at the entrance to the woods where the path forked. She had walked along to the left for a short distance a few days before, but Brad led her to the right.

As they walked, he explained how the boundary dispute had developed. Several times — whenever one of his ancestors found himself in financial difficulties — Brad told her, he had sold off a piece of property. The three hundred acres of The Queen's Grant had been the last parcel sold to one Benjamin Rowe, and the owner at that time, Peter Bradford, had always regretted the deal. The feud about the boundary had begun then.

"Considering the amount of acreage involved, you wouldn't think two acres were worth arguing about, would you?" Brad commented. "Watch out for that steppingstone — it isn't steady. We don't have far to go now."

"I'm enjoying the walk," Anne told him. But she could not tell him how she actually felt: the feeling of elation and pride as she looked up at the tall trees on either side of the path; the thrill of the knowledge that this ground, these trees, the brook they had just crossed and even the thorny bushes and undergrowth were *hers*!

If she had been alone, she thought she might have whooped for joy and danced along the path. But Brad would have thought her foolish; he was used to the idea of owning property. So instead she said practically:

"I marvel we are able to find a path at all, these bushes are so aggressive." Brad lifted a branch out of her way and held it aside.

"Yes, the land is fertile," Brad agreed, "but the woods haven't exactly been neglected all these years. Every so often most of the land owners in this area sell some of the lumber. They ask a woodsman who knows how to mark the trees, so that the 'mother' trees are left. Then, too, there's an old character in Glenbrook who makes a living cutting back the underbrush. I think he's working on our place right now."

They were climbing steadily as the road curved around a hill which, Anne thought, might easily qualify as a mountain as far as she was concerned. Brad looked back at her and came to a halt.

"Take a minute to catch your breath," he said, patting a fallen tree trunk. "After you've been here awhile, you'll be sprinting along this path without stopping."

"I doubt it," Anne said as she sat down and drew a deep breath. "I'm just not the mountain-climbing type."

"You wouldn't seem the type to run a nursing home, either," Brad commented, looking down at her.

"A *rest* home," Anne corrected him.

"Is there a difference?"

"Yes, quite a difference. A nursing home must be in a new building built especially for that purpose. It requires a nursing staff and almost the same facilities as a hospital. But a rest home is for those older people who find, through no fault of their own, that they are homeless. They may not require nursing care, but they do need comfortable surroundings, and there should be a doctor on call."

"Does Dr. Hewitt like the idea?"

"He's going to find out exactly how to go about it. As a matter of fact, he told me he had long wanted to see a rest home set up in this county."

"I like the way your eyes shine when you talk about what you want to do," Brad said. "And now, perhaps we'd better get along to those disputed acres."

He had not been kidding when he had said the going might be rough, Anne told him as they left the path and pushed their way through the heavy undergrowth. Some of the bushes were higher than her head, and twice she had to stop because her hair became tangled in the branches. The second time it happened, Brad came back and helped her to get free.

"I should have worn a bandana," Anne said as he carefully unwound a strand of hair.

"Your hair is so beautiful I wouldn't like to see you cover it. But you should learn to duck," he added with a grin.

When they came to the spot where the boundary was disputed, it looked no less wild to Anne than the ground they had just walked over. However, Brad pointed out a tree with a rusty barbed wire running through the trunk; the wire had been fastened to the tree when it was only a sapling, he explained. Then the tree had grown around it, so that now the wire ran through the middle of the trunk. After another scramble through the brush, they came upon a carefully pyramided pile of boulders.

"Are these the 'markers' of my property line?" Anne asked. "They seem sort of — well, unprofessional."

"These are what the Bradfords call the markers of your property line in this section," Brad replied. "As you see, they are very old, and those early surveyors used anything they found handy. About two hundred yards toward our place are the markers Benjamin Rowe set up. They are all uniform. They are lengths of pipe driven into the ground and evenly spaced. Shall we inspect them?"

"No," Anne said hastily. "I'll take your word for it. I gather that when Benjamin Rowe had the land surveyed after he bought it, he simply disregarded these first markers, or he thought they were wrong."

As she spoke, she thought there was a movement near a large juniper bush that had grown into a forest of bristling greenery. Brad did not seem to notice it.

"Benjamin Rowe simply took an

extra hunk of land," he said grimly.

"So you want to carry on the feud?"

"No, but you've got to admit these first markers tell their own story."

"I admit nothing . . . " Anne's voice trailed off as she looked again toward the juniper bush. It was probably only her imagination, but a man's face seemed to materialize among the branches. The skin was as brown as a mummy's and stretched tightly over the bones; white hair straggled down; the bright eyes looked as sharp as an animal's. For one wild moment, Anne thought she was psychic and had conjured up the ghost of an early settler.

"Brad," she said tremulously, "do you — do you see — " And then the face split into a hideous, toothless grin. Anne screamed, and screamed again.

Instantly Brad's arms were around her, and she buried her face against his shoulder. As if from a distance, she heard him say sternly:

"Cocky Biermann, you old devil,

come out from behind that juniper. Do you want to scare this girl out of her wits? I hired you to cut the underbrush; not to frighten an angel!"

★ ★ ★

Bob Rowe was waiting when Anne went down to dinner that night. She would have preferred to have all meals in the breakfast room, since there were just the two of them, but Bob had decreed they must eat dinner in the formal dining room. Mary Stone of course agreed to whatever Bob said; she had simply disregarded Anne's suggestion.

She would have to have a showdown with Bob Rowe, Anne knew, but she was reluctant to start an argument or possible court action; it was hard for her to live in an atmosphere of hostility. Although it was the coward's way out, Anne had decided to let the present situation drift along as it was. But Bob's air of ownership was hard to take at times.

"I had quite a lively discussion with Butch this morning on the subject of Indians," she said as she took her seat at the table and started on the fruit cup already in place. "It seems his grandfather told him there are arrowheads to be found for the looking, and that's his number one project."

"We're pretty lucky his heroes are Indians this year," Bob said genially, "and that he's interested in their hunting activities; not in scalping."

"Horror! I never thought of that," Anne exclaimed.

"Probably his grandfather emphasized the hunting angle. Last year, Mary Stone tells me, Butch was all for pirates, and they had to keep the kitchen knives under lock and key. He was also given to shouting: 'Walk the plank!' at odd moments. He came up behind Mrs. Stone one day just as she was taking a pie out of the oven, and she dropped it. Only a grandmother could forgive that."

"Boys will be boys," Anne commented

as Mrs. Stone brought in the roast duck and set it in front of Bob Rowe. The housekeeper made no remark, but her manner indicated she considered Bob the head of the house and her boss. As if he divined Anne's irritation, Bob said lightly:

"I like to carve. It is one of my many talents." He smiled as Mary Stone brought in apple sauce and whipped potatoes and she smiled fondly at him before returning to the kitchen.

"You do carve very nicely," Anne said as he gave her the plate. She was determined to keep up the friendly tone of the conversation. The next minute she forgot her resolution.

"Did you have a nice walk in the woods with our neighbor, Bradford? Mrs. Stone tells me you looked upset when you came back."

"Are you paying Mary Stone to spy on me?" Anne demanded.

"Now, now," Bob said soothingly. "I only asked Mrs. Stone where you were. There was something I wanted to tell you about the inventory. Then tonight, when you were late to dinner, she was worried you might not feel well."

The explanation was plausible, and Anne had to accept it. She told him about inspecting the boundary markers and the sudden and frightening appearance of Cocky Biermann. Bob Rowe was all sympathy; he had seen the village character. He took a dim view of the boundary dispute, however, and said it seemed a little late to bring up the matter.

"Brad is also giving a dinner party for me this Saturday at the Park-Savoy," Anne told him. "And you're invited."

"Say, maybe Brad isn't such a bad guy after all," he said with a grin. "Sure, I'll come. Is he inviting Cynthia Boynton, too?"

"Yes, he is." Anne was surprised at the question. "Do you know her? What is she like?"

Bob Rowe grinned. "I've met her,

and she's quite a girl. She's very beautiful, with black hair, white skin — very white skin — and a good figure. Yes, she's quite a girl!"

Anne wondered about the circumstances of the meeting, but she would not give Bob the satisfaction of asking how it had happened.

Cynthia Boynton was a debutante from St. Louis, Bob told her, here on vacation for a few weeks before flying on to Paris. There was a lively young crowd at the Park-Savoy, and she was on the go every minute. Anne also learned Cindy was an excellent swimmer, played a fast game of tennis and danced like a professional.

Bob told her all this with admiration, but with no indication that the debutante was of interest to him romantically. Anne wondered at this; from what he said, Cynthia Boynton sounded as if she liked a conquest, especially of someone handsome and charming.

"Brad is inviting Dr. Hewitt, too," Anne said. "he's going to help me establish this place as a rest home, you know."

Bob frowned, but he did not pursue the subject. Then, in a second, he was smiling again.

"We'll have a good time, I'm sure," he said, "except perhaps for Cindy. I take it you are Brad's guest of honor?"

"Yes, I am. But why do you say that about Cindy?"

"Because Cindy won't like it. She has marked Charles Hamilton Bradford as her own, and she doesn't take kindly to competition!"

6

FOR his dinner party welcoming Anne Carter to Glenbrook, Bradford had hired the Hollywood Room at the mountain-top Park-Savoy. Strictly speaking, it was not a room, but had only walls and no roof; it was open to the sky. For this occasion a rose-pink canopy had been put up.

Built out at the side of the third floor of the hotel, it offered by day a magnificent view of the countryside; the end wall was almost entirely a picture window. At night the panorama was different: lights glowed like static fireflies in the village below, twinkling from the impressive homes that dotted the rolling hills and outlined the highway in the distance.

The Hollywood Room took its name from the murals covering three of the

walls. They were blown-up repro-
ductions of scenes from famous movies
which had later been painted over
in spectacular colors. They made a
striking background for the eight dinner
tables, seating six guests each. Deep
pink tablecloths disappeared between
borders of silver lamé at the sides and
ends; pink carnations were massed high
at the center of each table.

As she went into the room, Anne
knew she looked well, but her feelings
were all mixed up. Dr. Steve Atkinson
had appeared unexpectedly that Saturday
afternoon with the intention of spending
the weekend. Anne had had no choice
but to call Brad and explain she had
a guest. Brad had instantly invited
him to the party, but Anne still felt
embarrassed about it.

Her short dinner dress was of
turquoise silk crepe; it had a plain,
sleeveless bodice with a boat neckline
and a scant skirt, attached at the
waist with meager gathers. Her carved
turquoise earrings had been her mother's.

Anne was glad she had taken such pains dressing when she entered the Hollywood Room with Brad and Steve. Cynthia Boynton was already there, talking with Bob Rowe. Cynthia was wearing pink organza, the ankle-length skirt made of many layers of the filmy material. A necklace of diamonds sparkled at the base of her long, slender throat. When she saw Anne and her escorts come in, Cynthia came over at once.

"Hello, Steve," she said in a throaty voice. "I've missed seeing you this last year."

"Do you two know each other?" asked Anne.

"You could put it that way, darling," Cynthia drawled, and held up her face to be kissed. "St. Louis is our mutual home town."

Anne enjoyed Steve's embarrassment as he pecked at Cynthia's cheek; it served him right for not having let her know he was coming to Glenbrook this weekend.

The guests at the other tables were seated, and the laughter and repartee already in full swing justified Bob's description of them as a 'lively' crowd. They applauded with gusto as Anne walked over to the head table.

Brad, as host, sat at one end of the table, with Anne at his right and Cynthia at his left. Dr. Hewitt had been given the other end of the table; his 'date' was a white-haired widow whom he introduced as an old friend. At the doctor's left was a pert young redhead named Maggi, evidently invited as a last-minute partner for Steve. But Anne saw Cynthia adroitly switch place cards before they sat down; Steve sat next to her, and Bob Rowe was between Anne and Maggi.

Bob is right, Anne thought to herself. Cynthia is not only beautiful; she is also a fast-thinking girl.

Most of the men, like the host, wore conservative dark summer suits. But Bob Rowe was resplendent in a white silk jacket, worn with formal black trousers and a black bow tie. He seemed to enjoy being conspicuously handsome.

Making dinner conversation with Bob Rowe was not Anne's idea of a gala occupation, but with Cynthia chattering gaily to both Brad and Steve, giving Bob the silent treatment would have seemed noticeably rude. She cast around in her mind for something to say and came up with nothing brighter than:

"Lovely view, isn't it?"

"Righto, Anne. A marvelous view!" Bob said enthusiastically, fastening his eyes on Cynthia. Instantly, Cindy picked up the cue, leaned toward Steve, and stage-whispered:

"From this angle — likewise!"

"What I'd like," said Steve, also sotto voce, "is to see more of Glenbrook."

"I'd love to show you around," returned Cynthia, her husky voice making it seem like a romantic rendevouz.

Brad abruptly rose and, tapping on

his water glass with a fork, commanded the attention of all his guests. The soup course had been removed, and the record player was suddenly stilled. All conversation stopped.

"Ladies and gentleman," said Brad, "I have the honor to welcome Miss Anne Rowe Carter, formerly of New York and currently of Glenbrook. She's the new and decorative owner of that fine old estate, The Queen's Grant."

Applause greeted the announcement. Brad extended his hand to Anne, and she rose and faced the crowd of friendly faces.

"Thank you," she murmured. "Thank you so much."

"Speech!" someone shouted. "Speech!"

"I don't know what to say." Anne spread her hands in a helpless gesture. Everybody laughed as if this were a witty remark. "The only time I've been applauded before," she went on, "was when I was capped and the audience clapped for each of the graduating class in turn. I felt very proud then, and I feel mighty proud now." She sat down, and now the prolonged applause was mingled with wolf whistles.

Bob Rowe caught her hand and squeezed it under cover of the table. She smiled at him but pulled her hand away as quickly as she could. Turning to Brad, she said: "I was never so surprised and at a loss for words in my life!"

"Yeah?" drawled Cynthia. "Hear hear!" She leaned toward Steve. "What do you bet our little Anne had that speech ready ahead of time, in case she was called on? Probably she's got a million of 'em," she said insolently.

But this was going too far for Bob Rowe. "You hush, jealous girl! Just for that, I'm going to kiss Anne."! He bent quickly toward her, but Anne was too fast; she turned her face aside so that he kissed the turquoise earring.

"If at first you don't succeed — " jeered Cynthia, but she turned her attention to Brad.

The music began again and the next

course was served — the main dish, veal with orange sauce. When this course was cleared away, there was a pause, while the music stopped and Brad rose as before.

"I was going to hire a few entertainers for this gala," he said, "but then it occurred to me that with all you talented people on hand, it would not be necessary. The guest of honor will be excused; she has already had her say. But everybody else in alphabetical order will be required to stand up and tell us about a new discovery — a book, a play, a person — he or she has made recently."

Shrieks of protest greeted this announcement. Brad held up his hand.

"Anyone who refuses to cooperate will get no dessert," he informed them. He consulted a list on the table before him. "I call first upon our guest from New York — Dr. Steve Atkinson."

"I don't know what kinds of desserts they serve in this place," Steve said, "but I'm not to miss whatever it is.

So here goes." He took a deep breath and looked directly at Anne.

"I'm glad you gave this party to introduce the world's prettiest nurse to Glenbrook. However," Steve added with a grin, "remember *I* discovered Nurse Anne Carter first. She's *mine*!"

Trust Steve to act as if he owned her, Anne thought. She saw Brad's lips tighten, but he waited until the applause died down and then called on Cynthia Boynton. Instead of standing in her place, Cynthia danced a few twist steps, the layers of her pink organza skirt fluttering around her like the wings of a butterfly, and brought up in the center of the floor.

"I've discovered a new record." She called to the man handling the records, and he nodded as she named it. When he had put it on the machine, Cynthia whirled into an exotic dance which had her audience applauding even before she finished. It was an astonishing exhibition of grace and skill for a non-professional. Anne said so, when

Cindy returned to the table.

Cynthia gave her a frosty smile. "I've been invited to turn professional," she said. "Maybe I will — just for kicks!"

When Brad's turn came, he outlined a movie comedy he said he had seen; no one else had ever heard of it. It was a hilarious jumble of the plots of several comedies, and everyone roared with laughter, frequently drowning out his words so that he had to repeat his lines.

There was an interruption when the salad arrived, and afterward the entertainment again proceeded briskly. The guests described their 'discoveries' — books, plays, places of interest and people. Some were serious about their finds; others burlesqued them. But nobody refused to contribute to the unusual entertainment.

After the dessert for which everyone had worked so energetically — baked Alaska — had been served and eaten, the tables were removed from the room. Some chairs were ranged along the walls for the spectators, and dancing began.

Anne and Brad were standing together waiting for a new record to slip into place, when Cynthia came up. Insinuating herself between them, she clasped her arms around Brad's neck and, the instant the music started, danced him onto the floor.

The hot color rose to Anne's cheeks as she stared after them. Now why did I let her get away with that? she scolded herself. But Steve was at her side immediately, and from then on she had her choice of partners.

Anne exerted herself to give each partner the impression that dancing with him made the evening for her. Whenever Brad looked her way, she contrived to be laughing, or gazing up admiringly into the eyes of the man with her.

When she was dancing with Bob Rowe, she repeated the admiring glance upward and felt his arm tighten about her.

"That's the way I like to have a girl

look at me," he whispered, making sure that his lips brushed her ear.

"Think nothing of it," Anne said airily.

"Ah, but I do!" Bob declared. "Tell me, Anne — do I have a chance against your doctor beau?"

Anne evaded the question by stopping in front of the spot where Dr. Mark Hewitt was sitting with his partner. He smiled at her benignly, but his glance was sharp as he looked at Bob.

"I was very glad to meet you tonight, Rowe," the doctor said. "I understand you claim to be the grandson of Anne Rowe."

"I *am* the grandson, sir," Bob retorted.

"Oh?" Dr. Hewitt paused for a moment and then said: "Anne Rowe was a good friend of mine, years ago."

Anne looked at him curiously; this was exactly opposite from what the doctor had told her in private. Then she glanced at Bob. There was a muscle throbbing in his temple, and it took an effort for him to smile. When he did speak, however, his voice was smooth.

"She was a wonderful woman, sir. Shall we continue our dance, Anne?"

"By all means do," the doctor said. "I only wish I could dance with our beautiful guest of honor. But I have to content myself nowadays with sedentary pleasures. Don't be surprised, Anne, if I come on a house call one of these days. I have some information I'd like to discuss with you."

"Come any time," Anne said cordially as Bob whirled her away.

"You and I will have to talk one of these days," Bob said sadly. "Your doctor pal all but said I was a fraud, and I don't like it. I'll show you the proof."

Later, when Brad finally cut in on a dance, Anne was still worried about what Bob had said. However, in a moment she forgot about it. After they had danced a few steps, Brad said quietly:

"Why have you been avoiding me all evening?"

"*Avoiding* you!" Anne said coldly. "I was under the impression you danced away from *me* — with Cynthia Boynton."

"Cindy makes up her own rules as she goes along," Brad said lightly. "Anyway, your Doctor Steve made it pretty clear that he considered you his fiancée."

"Steve had no right to say what he did," Anne said hotly. "Oh, Brad, don't let's snap at each other. It's a beautiful party; I had a wonderful time, and I do thank you for it. But in a way I feel like Cinderella at the ball. When the clock strikes, I have to forget the magic and the glamour and get back to my problems."

There was a small reception room just down the hall, Brad said, where they could talk in comparative privacy. It was deserted when they went in, and Anne, suddenly tired from all the excitement, sank gratefully into an armchair. She didn't know whether she was doing the right thing or not, but she knew she had to have advice.

Brad pulled up a chair close to hers, and she began with her first impression of the man who claimed to be her aunt's grandson. Brad had heard about the claim before, but he had assumed Anne considered it valid. She told him about the ring he said Aunt Anne had given him, and the other 'proofs' which he was going to present to her. Brad listened without comment until she finished. Then he said in a puzzled tone:

"Why haven't you haled him into court long since?"

Anne felt tears stinging her eyelids and blinked them back. What if Brad, too, had been taken in by Bob's charm?

"Brad, I'm a miserable coward. Maybe his proofs are legitimate, I don't know. But if he can tie up the estate, it may take years to set up the rest home I have in mind. I just can't seem to think straight any more."

Brad said thoughtfully, "I never did like the fellow," and Anne felt as if a weight had been lifted from her shoulders. "Tonight I thought he got way out of line. But proving he's a crook is something else again. You say he comes from Chicago?"

"I believe that's true. Aunt Anne died in Chicago, and he claims she had gone there to see him."

Brad nodded as if satisfied. "That simplifies things," he said, and when Anne looked questioning, he added: "I have a good friend who is now a noted criminal lawyer in Chicago. I'll fly out there and ask him if he can get any information on this man. If he's a phoney, Jerry Linden will soon find out."

The warm glow she felt at Brad's promise to help lasted through the rest of the evening. She wondered why she had ever doubted he had been fooled by Bob's charm; he had made his dislike particularly clear tonight.

It was not until she was back home and alone in her room that she thought of the answer. Brad had said Bob Rowe had been 'way out of line' at the party. He had resented Bob's attentions to Cynthia Boynton!

7

ANNE would have preferred to put off the showdown with Bob Rowe, at least until after Brad had time to go to Chicago, but he insisted upon talking with her the next afternoon. He found her in the conservatory, one of her favorite spots, and came to the point at once.

"As I told you last night, Anne, I don't like your friend Dr. Mark Hewitt, or his sly insinuations. I have my mother's marriage license, and her letter to me and my grandmother's ring. They are all here in this box. Shall we look at them."

"I don't see what would be gained by that," Anne objected. "I have no legal training."

"You're doing all right without it," Bob answered, but he softened his retort with a grin. "You've got Dr.

Hewitt all excited about setting up a rest home, and you've got me taking inventory . . . "

"Inventory was your idea," Anne reminded him. "And if I may say so, you're not doing a very speedy job."

"You want me to rush it?" Bob Rowe demanded. Then again he softened his manner. "Don't let's quarrel, my dear. I've done all but five rooms on the inventory, and the few pieces I've checked, such as the dining room table, are the real McCoy. You'll get a fortune from the sale of the furniture alone."

"But I don't want to sell."

"Oh, be realistic, Anne."

"It's my property; you can't tell me what to do with it."

"You're acting like a child."

"I'll act any way I want to!"

Bob Rowe spread his hands in a gesture of resignation. "I can't control you, of course. But if I may point out one fact, dear cousin — "

"Second cousin — *perhaps*!"

"All right, second cousin. Even if you should establish a rest home here, you would be foolish to keep the furniture, or the glassware collection, or the paintings, or many of the other valuable pieces. In an institution, oak or maple — cheap stuff — is what you need for the inmates."

Anne resented the word 'inmates,' but she decided on a change of tactics. This was no time to explain to Bob that she was dreaming of a home where those who stayed would be guests and where those who appreciated fine surroundings would be able to enjoy them in their later years. He would not even try to understand her point of view.

"Bob, I can't discuss any of this with you today. Steve has to leave this afternoon, and meanwhile, I must make like a hostess."

"Yes, of course. But I hope you will think over what I've said. By the way, where is Steve? Sleeping late?"

"No, he's gone to the Park-Savoy

to pick up Cynthia Boynton. Seems her brother was an old college chum, and he used to call her 'Little Sister.'" Bob looked skeptical, but made no comment. "They'll probably be here soon."

"Some other time, then. But meanwhile, just one more word on the furnishings: how about asking Bradford to buy them? He might be interested; they're just right for the export-import business he and his father have established."

"Have you spoken to him about it?" Anne demanded.

Bob shook his head. "I have a feeling our neighbor doesn't like me. Not that it matters, but I think he'd be more receptive if the suggestion came from you."

She would think it over, Anne promised, determined not to be pressured into a prolonged discussion. Meanwhile, she told Bob, she would have to go upstairs and dress.

An hour later, Anne surveyed herself

critically in the mirror as she fastened the belt of the crisp cotton — white, with green leaves scattered lavishly over it. Her light tan was becoming; her eyes sparkled. Anne Rowe Carter did not look at all like the weary nurse who had first come to The Queen's Grant.

Then she heard a car drive up and Steve's baritone, a girl's answering voice, laughter. Anne ran downstairs.

Steve was standing beside his car, one arm around Cynthia Boynton. As Anne came down the steps toward them, he attempted to take his arm away from Cynthia, but she caught his wrist and held his arm firmly around her waist. He would have had to pull away in order to get free. Instead, he reached out for Anne with his other arm, pulled her to him and kissed her lightly on the top of her head.

"Oh, two-timing me, are you?" Cynthia chided.

"But you can still be his 'Little Sister,'" Anne retorted.

Cynthia looked at her with narrowed eyes. "Does it matter to you?" she drawled in her husky voice.

Anne shrugged. "Not at all. Shall we go inside?"

She pulled away and led them into the house and toward the living room. Cynthia linked her arm firmly in Steve's, and as they came into the room she pulled him toward a love seat and pushed him down, seating herself beside him.

"We have *so* much to talk about!" Cynthia put her head on Steve's shoulder. "Steve — do you remember — ?" She related some incident that had taken place in St. Louis. Steve, unable to resist, joined in the reminiscence and added a few comments of his own. The room rang with Cindy's laughter.

Anne felt like saying: 'Don't mind me; I'm only your hostess.' But she sternly repressed the impulse.

Brad's arrival created a sensation. Steve stood up to shake hands with him and, under cover of walking across the room with the newcomer, seized the opportunity to find himself a chair without arms, instead of going back to the love seat. Anne wasn't certain Steve had chosen the chair with a view of keeping Cindy from perching on the chair arm, but it had that result. Steve stood beside it, waiting for Anne and touching the back of the chair next to it as an invitation to her to sit there.

Anne's eyes sparkled; she could do a little 'remembering' of her own. It was easy to engage Steve in talk of the hospital which had been 'theirs' in New York. They were soon chattering away with only an occasional over-the-shoulder remark to the others.

Mary Stone brought in little sandwiches and iced coffee and announced she would be glad to bring a highball 'for the doctor', if he desired. Steve said no, the coffee was fine, and grinned at Anne, who knew he seldom drank anything but an occasional glass of wine with his dinner.

Then Anne had to show Steve the house and grounds, and he admitted to being greatly impressed. By this time, Bob Rowe had joined the group and, to Anne's annoyance, insisted upon making a show of close friendship with her. Steve looked at him sharply once or twice, particularly when Bob, with a possessive gesture took Anne's arm with what she said to herself was a 'silly smirk on his face.'

Everybody was invited to stay for dinner, and everyone accepted with alacrity, Steve included. Anne was surprised but pleased that he was having a good time. Perhaps it meant he was beginning to see things from her point of view!

"My arrival in New York an hour or two later than I planned won't make any real difference," Steve explained. "I have no appointments before ten tomorrow."

"Why don't you arrange to come up and stay for a while?" Anne said impulsively. "I'm sure it would do you

110

good to get away from New York and, frankly, I'd like to have you."

"That would be a fine idea," Steve agreed. "It seems to me you and Bob Rowe are getting a shade too friendly. Perhaps I should come up and run interference."

"Bob can be most annoying," Anne told him. "But at the party last night, and today, he was simply putting on an act. He knows how I feel about him and his claim of being the long-lost grandson of Aunt Anne."

"But he must have some proof. Why don't you ask to see it?"

Bob offered to show her his 'proofs,' Anne admitted, but she didn't want to get into a serious discussion until she had legal advice.

"The sooner you take action the better," Steve said pontifically, "because you must be prepared to find his claims will stand up in court, no matter what you think. No use building your hopes too high, especially on this rest home idea."

"You'd be pleased if it turned out Bob is okay?" Anne asked.

"You might say 'yes' more quickly," Steve answered. "And that's all I really care about."

"But what about Cindy Boynton?" Anne teased. "You might break her heart!"

"Cindy will always find consolation," Steve said dryly. "She's the type."

After dinner they went to the games room and danced to the latest records. Although Aunt Anne had been over fifty when she died, she had enjoyed popular music, and the record collection was good. Cynthia apparently decided to divide her time between Steve and Bob Rowe. She was grateful when Bob decided to call it an evening and went to his room.

"We can sit this one out, if you like," Steve offered. "You must be tired."

"No, I like to dance," Anne said. "But you have a long drive ahead of you. Let's sit over here for a few minutes anyway."

"Going back to what I was saying before dinner," Steve began, "I wonder if you aren't being a little stubborn about Bob Rowe. Some of those anecdotes he told at dinner were most amusing, and he seemed to make a play for Cindy as well as you. I guess it's just his line. Anyway, you should consider a compromise, in my opinion."

"You find him charming, too," Anne said bitterly.

"Anne, you've got to admit he is good-looking, intelligent and charming — at least as far as women are concerned. Why won't you admit the possibility you could be wrong?"

"My mother used to quote an old proverb that she would rather be swindled by a knave than a fool," Anne said tartly. "I'd rather not be swindled by anybody. Shall we dance?"

Before her guests left, Anne took Cynthia up to her room to freshen up. Steve would drop her at the Park-Savoy on his way back to New York; Brad would drive back to his own place alone. Cindy was in high spirits; evidently she felt the evening had been well worth-while.

"So you and Steve have something going for each other," she said as she applied fresh makeup before Anne's dressing table. "Well, well, will wonders never cease!"

"What do you mean by that?" Anne demanded.

"Oh, nothing special," Cindy said airily; "just that when I knew him in St. Louis, he seemed more the social type. His family has money, you know. Timber, I think. Anyway, none of us ever thought he'd be interested in a nurse."

"What's wrong with him liking a nurse?"

Cynthia met Anne's eyes in the mirror, and she smiled. "Do I have to spell it out for you, darling? There's nothing wrong with it. Only you hear so much talk about people marrying other people with suitable and similar backgrounds . . . "

"You sound as if you still thought of Steve in a romantic way. And when you first came in, I thought you acted that way, too."

Cindy paused in the act of applying a brilliant lipstick and swung around to face her hostess. Her beauty was undeniable, Anne thought. The velvety white of her skin, the perfect wings of her brows above dark eyes and the wide generous curves of her mouth gave Cynthia a regal beauty.

"If it will make you any happier, my dear," she drawled, "Steve and I decided to call it quits over a year ago. But surely you are not so naïve as to think you can let any man be sure of you before the wedding ring is on your finger? Oh, no! Not you. You've imported this Bob Rowe to make Steve jealous, just as I find it convenient to have Steve around when I am dating Brad."

Anne was repelled by Cynthia's cynical attitude toward love and marriage, but she did not want to discuss her real feelings toward Bob Rowe.

"I've invited Steve to come here for a vacation," she told Cindy as she again busied herself with her lipstick. "He said he would try to arrange it."

"Good!" Cynthia approved. "Maybe we could double-date a few times. I understand you can rent horses — riding horses — from a stable in Glenbrook, and there's quite a nice lake nearby. They have sailboats. Do you sail?"

Anne admitted she never had, but she expressed her willingness to accompany the party.

"Good!" Cindy said again. "Let me know when Steve is coming up, and we'll work out a real vacation schedule. By the way," she said as she got up to leave, "how long are you going to be here, Anne? Bob Rowe said something about you being here just long enough to sell the place."

"I have no intention of selling."

"You haven't! Don't tell me you're

going to marry Steve and then retire him up here."

"I'm going to set up a rest home — a place where people can be happy and comfortable and well cared for . . . " Anne broke off as she saw Cindy's expression.

"What a revolting idea!" Cindy said finally. "Does Brad know about this?"

Anne nodded.

"Well, I'm sure he doesn't approve," Cindy said acidly. "Imagine the Bradfords having an institution next door to their beautiful estate. I think you must have been carried away by your aunt's legacy. There are some things you just don't do!"

After everyone had gone, Anne sat in the living room staring into space. Cynthia Boynton's words had hurt. It was almost useless to tell herself that a spoiled debutante, whose life was lived in a meaningless round of pleasure, could not possibly appreciate the wonderful feeling that enveloped you when you were of service to your fellow men. Cindy's life was a selfish, shallow existence; she knew no other.

Yet Florence Nightingale herself had been a social butterfly, Anne thought. She could have lived as Cindy lived, surrounded by luxury and pleasure. Instead, she had dedicated herself to nursing and to helping others. How richly rewarding her life had been!

As Anne turned off the living room lights and prepared to go upstairs, she felt immeasurably better. She could not hope to equal the service started by 'The Lady with the Lamp.' but she could do her small share to make the world a little brighter.

8

IT was hard to live in a state of indecision, Anne was thinking a few days later. Bob Rowe had not tried to discuss his 'proofs' again, but she knew he was thinking of them whenever he spoke to her. Late in the afternoon, she was so restless she threw down the book she was reading and told Mary Stone she was going for a drive.

Anne drove for an hour, taking any road that appealed to her, and finally found she had been circling and was headed back toward Glenbrook. But the idea of a drive had been good; she felt much calmer and more relaxed.

When she reached The Queen's Grant, Anne went at once to the kitchen. She had an outsize lollipop she had stopped and bought for Butch. Mary Stone was alone there, busy preparing the dinner.

Anne waved the lollipop. "Where's Butch?"

"Around somewhere," said Mary Stone, stirring something in a saucepan vigorously. "Probably with Jim in the garage. Jim's fixin' something out there."

Anne went out the side door and around the path to the converted barn.

"Gimme a bite?" said a voice behind her. Anne turned and met Bob's mischievous grin.

"Have you seen Butch?" she asked.

"I've only just come back," Bob told her. "Have you mislaid Butch?"

"Of course not! I'm looking for him so that I can give him this lollipop. Mary Stone thinks he may be with Jim in the garage."

"Yoo-hoooo!" With his hands cupped around his mouth, Bob Rowe emitted a piercing yodel that made Anne jump. "That ought to bring him," he said complacently.

"An Indian war-whoop would bring

him faster," said Anne. "He's still on the Indian kick."

"I know. Didn't I buy him a bow and arrow set? He's mad about it."

"Before you bought it, I wish you'd made him a target to shoot at," said Anne. "Yesterday he shot off my sun hat when I was out in the garden."

"He *did*!" Bob exclaimed. "There's marksmanship for you! I gave him the set only yesterday morning."

"He wasn't aiming at my hat," said Anne severely. "Butch told me afterward he had been aiming at the iron deer on the lawn. But he might have shot my eye out."

She had reached the barn by this time, Bob right behind her, though she had purposely hastened her steps, trying to outdistance him. Jim Stone stuck his head out of the doorway.

"Is Butch with you?" Anne asked.

"Haven't seen him." Jim Stone seemed unconcerned. "Playin' in the woods, likely."

"Alone?"

"He doesn't go far in," Jim explained. "I tell him there's Indians in there, waitin' to grab him."

"And torture him and burn him at the stake, I suppose. Scare a child half to death — that's sound training for you!" Bob observed in an undertone. But Jim heard him.

"Scare that young 'un? Can't be done," he said firmly. "Butch doesn't believe me, anyway. Tough, the kid is. That's the way he ought to be."

"Let's you and I go into the woods and look for him," suggested Bob, looking at Anne. "Then if he's lost — "

"Why don't you get lost yourself?" she demanded. "I'm going into the house — and stop following me."

At dinner time Butch still had not returned. Mary Stone rang the big brass bell she kept on the back porch to summon the youngster when he wandered away. But there was still no sign of him when they sat down at the table. It began to grow dark earlier than usual.

"Thunderstorm coming up," said the housekeeper.

Anne laid down her fork abruptly. "I'm going to look for Butch!" she cried, and pushed her chair back.

"No," said Bob Rowe, also getting up. "You don't know the woods. You couldn't find your own way, let alone find the boy. I'll get Jim Stone to call some of the neighbors; we'll make up a search party."

Within half an hour a group of men had gathered in the yard, all carrying flashlights. Jim Stone carried a shotgun. "Three shots will tell you the boy is found," he told his wife. Anne watched them go.

"No good just staring out the window," said Mary Stone practically when, after the men had disappeared into the woods, Anne still stood at the kitchen window. "Go look at television or read or somethin'. Take your mind off it. They'll find him soon."

Anne went up to her room, but she could not settle down to anything.

She was tortured by thoughts that came crowding into her mind. Butch might have tripped or fallen; be lying somewhere unable to move. He might have encountered a poisonous snake. Hadn't someone mentioned a place called Rattlesnake Hill, only a few miles away? And there must be wildcats about; even porcupines could be dangerous.

She was on the balcony outside her room when the storm broke. Rain pelted the leaves of an overhanging tree as if with bullets. New lightning split the sky almost before the echoes of the last thunderclap had died away.

Anne retreated to her room, leaving the French doors open. But after a moment, when a stream of water began to make its way toward the rug, she had to close both doors and windows. She shuddered uncontrollably as the lightning snaked across the sky and the thunder shook the house. She did not remember having been frightened by a storm before, but then she had never stood safe under a roof while, in her mind, a series of pictures unreeled like a movie. She saw a small boy knocked senseless by a great branch from a lightning-shattered tree, his head gashed, his legs pinned to the ground . . .

It was too much to endure. The rain was lessening, or she wanted to think it was. Anne pulled on boots, slipped her arms into her raincoat which, luckily, had a hood, and stuffed one pocket with a sweater and a warm scarf. In the other she put a flashlight and, as a final inspiration, the lollipop, still in its wrapper, which had been lying on her bureau. Outside her door, she stood listening for a moment. The noise of the storm had died away, and she could hear no sound in the house. The men had not returned, then!

"Where are you going?" Anne had reached the bottom of the stairs when Mary Stone appeared suddenly in the doorway leading to the kitchen wing.

"I thought I'd look around a little," began Anne.

"Think you can find Butch when the men can't?" asked Mary Stone scornfully. "You're out of your mind." But Anne noticed the housekeeper's eyes were red and her cheeks were wet; she held back the sharp retort that sprang to her lips.

"I might," she murmured gently, and went out the front door. But even as she opened it, there was the sound of a shot.

"There!" Mary Stone cried. "They've found him! I told you they would. Might as well come back in and take off your boots."

A great wave of relief swept over Anne, and she followed Mary into the kitchen, where she slipped out of her raincoat and pulled off her boots. The housekeeper was crying again when she looked up.

"I'm so happy," she said brokenly. "And to think I was so mad when he broke the window with his arrow this afternoon! I told him I'd take the set away from him, but he grabbed the bow and arrow and ran."

"Did you see him later?" asked Anne.

"No," sobbed Mary Stone. "The last I saw of him he was running toward the woods. If anything has happened to him, I guess it's my fault." She wiped her eyes with a corner of her apron.

"You shouldn't blame yourself," said Anne, sorry for the woman. "After all, you couldn't let Butch shoot out the windows and not say a thing about it! Besides, they've found him now, so there's nothing to worry about."

For a while they sat in silence, waiting for the return of the search party with the boy.

"The poor kid must have got soaked through in the storm," said Anne finally, just to have something to say. "He ought to have some hot milk and a peanut butter sandwich or something like that when he gets home."

"Butch won't drink milk," said his grandmother.

"Cocoa, then," said Anne. "I'll make some."

"No," the housekeeper objected, "I'll make it. If anything gets me on edge, it's somebody messin' around my kitchen, burnin' holes in my pans."

"Goodness! You must take me for some kind of a nitwit, Mary Stone. Don't you think a nurse can be trusted to make a cup of cocoa without wrecking the kitchen?"

"Ain't takin' no chances," the housekeeper said. She went to the cupboard where her pans were kept. Anne couldn't trust herself not to reply to this, but before she could leave the kitchen, she heard voices outside the door.

"They're coming now." Anne flung the kitchen door wide. Jim Stone was being helped up the three steps to the kitchen porch.

"Jim, you're hurt!" Mary Stone

pushed Anne aside and ran to help her husband.

"Just a sprained ankle," said Jim. "Woods are full of mud holes after that downpour, and I slipped in one and turned my ankle. No use stayin' out. I can't help when I can't walk."

Between the neighbor who had brought him in and his wife, Jim was helped to a cushioned armchair by the kitchen window. Anne knelt beside him and, taking Jim's own jackknife, cut the laces of his high boot. She removed it as gently as possible, but every pull was to the accompaniment of loud cries from Jim. The ankle had already swelled alarmingly, she saw, when the boot was off at last.

"It doesn't seem to be broken," she said, "but Dr. Hewitt will have to decide that." She placed a cushion under the injured foot.

"I don't need no doctor for a turned ankle," Jim Stone said. "Bandage it up, and I'll be all right by tomorrow."

"You'll have a doctor look at

it," Anne said firmly. "I certainly won't bandage your ankle without knowing what's wrong with it!" Jim still grumbled and groaned, but Anne went to the telephone and called Dr. Hewitt. He was at home and agreed to come to The Queen's Grant at once.

"All this fuss about a turned ankle!" Jim protested.

Frank Dubois, the neighbor who had helped Jim home, announced he might as well be getting along.

"I think you'd better stay till the doctor has seen Jim," said Anne. "Maybe you can help get him to bed. If the ankle is broken, he'll have to go to the hospital, of course. But if the doctor finds it's a sprain, Jim is as well off at home."

Dr. Hewitt drove up soon afterward, his manner jovial as the housekeeper brought him into the kitchen.

"Nice goings-on," he said in mock reproof to Jim, "running around the woods at night. What were you doing, anyway?"

Mary Stone explained about the search for Butch. "But they should have brought him back by this time!" cried Anne suddenly. "We heard the gunshot — the one that told us he was found — quite a long while ago!"

Jim Stone shook his head. "You heard only one blast — not three. And that was an accident. My gun went of when I slipped into the mud hole. It's a good thing I didn't shoot myself. I could use the gun as a crutch, coming home."

"Then Butch hasn't been found yet!" Anne's face bright with hope before, was shadowed with fear once more.

"It's hard getting around in the woods after the storm," said Frank Dubois. "Even with flashlights, it's next to impossible to see more than a few feet at a time."

Anne said nothing; simply picked up her boots and raincoat and walked from the kitchen to the front of the house. She put them on and listened for a moment. The others were still talking about Jim's accident; no one would miss her immediately. Then she opened the front door, shut it behind her noiselessly and, avoiding the gravel path, walked across the grass. She looked back from time to time, but no one was following her and she made the edge of the woods, where the trees hid her, without discovery.

Maybe she couldn't find Butch, but she was going to try!

She located a path of sorts and followed it with difficulty. Twice her hood caught on a thorny branch. Finally, exasperated, she pulled it off and crumpled it into her pocket. As Frank Dubois had said, a flashlight was not a great deal of use.

Anne swung it in wide circles as she struggled on, calling: "Butch! Butch!" at intervals. But all she succeeded in doing was rousing the small denizens of the woods; they squeaked, squawked or fluttered at her approach. She hoped desperately that none of the wood folk would resent her intrusion enough to attack her.

Now the clouds were scattering, and at intervals the moon made a brief appearance. Its uncanny light added an eerie note to an already weird scene.

Where were the other searchers? Anne couldn't see or hear anything of them. They must be deep in the wood by this time. Perhaps she was foolish to go on; they must have been over the ground already. But no, the woods covered a wide area, and the searchers would have had to spread themselves out thinly. It would have been easy to overlook a small boy huddled in some hollow.

Presently she noticed many tree stumps. Woodcutters had been busy there. Then she found herself entangled in the top branches that had been lopped off a great tree. The woodsmen had taken the part of the tree they wanted — the trunk — and left the rest barring the path. By the time she had extricated herself, her raincoat was torn in several places. When Anne dropped the flashlight, and the light went off, she felt it was the last straw as she scrabbled around on her hands and knees looking for it among the spiky needles of the fallen pine tree.

After this, when she had found the flashlight and sighed with relief as she discovered it still worked, she proceeded more cautiously, threading her way around each mass of widespread boughs which marked the fall of a wood's giant.

On one of these excursions, while she was eying the reaching limbs and sodden dead leaves of what must have been an imposing tree, Anne stepped suddenly into what seemed to be a yielding hillock. It took her a moment to step back and realize that she had blundered into a pile of sawdust. Just beyond it she could see the remnants of a crude sawmill and a great water wheel. She swept the beam of her flashlight over the wheel and caught the unmistakable gleam of water below it.

Fearfully she drew near, testing every foothold before she put her weight on the ground. What if Butch had blundered into the millpond!

Shining her flashlight over the stagnant water, iridescent in its beam, Anne shuddered. It might not be deep, half overgrown as it was by weeds and bushes, but a small boy, his feet sinking in layers of mud at the bottom, could easily be trapped in those murky depths and pulled beneath the water's surface.

"*Butch!*" called Anne. "*Butch!*" But her voice sounded faint even to her own ears.

She did not expect an answer. When she did hear a voice, she turned so abruptly that her foot slipped and for a moment she thought she would topple into the water herself as the muddy edge gave way under her frantic scrambling. But she reached firm ground in the next second.

Had she heard a thin, childish voice saying, "Here!" or had she imagined it?

"Butch!" she called again, louder this time. Again she swung her flashlight in a wide arc, and now it revealed the figure of the small boy huddled on a tree stump in the shadows behind a few upright boards, all that remained of the mill's well. Anne stumbled and sloshed her way toward the boy.

"Shh-hh!" Butch admonished her. "You make too much noise. You're scarin' the fish in my pond. I was just going to shoot one." Then Anne noticed he had his bow and arrow in his hands and was aiming at the still pond. "I'm sure I saw a big fish," he grumbled, "but you've frightened it away."

Anne put her hand on the boy's wet hair and touched the wet shoulders of the cowboy shirt clinging to his back. "Everybody's been looking for you, Butch," she said gently. "Weren't you afraid, out here all alone in that thunderstorm?"

"Naw," said Butch, "who's afraid of a little rain? And if a bear or a wolf had come along, I had my bow and arrow. I'd have shot any old bear dead."

"Of course," said Anne. "But you must be hungry." She felt in her pocket for the lollipop, but the pocket had been torn half off by one of her encounters with thorny bushes. The lollipop had fallen out.

"We'd better go home and get something to eat," said Anne, taking Butch's hand.

"Awright," he said resignedly.

After a while, as they made their way home — and Anne found they hadn't been so deep in the woods after all — Butch observed with all the pride of an explorer:

"The name of that pond is Butch's Pond. It's named after me. You know, the way they name rivers and things after the men who discover them? I discovered that pond, didn't I?"

Anne put her arm around his shoulders and managed to give him a hug before he twisted away.

"Yes, that's what you did," said Anne. "But the best part is what you *didn't* do."

"What's that?" asked Butch.

"You didn't fall in," said Anne.

9

TIME hung heavy on Anne's hands. Charles Bradford although he had offered to help, did not appear or call her; she wondered if perhaps he had regretted his offer to go to Chicago and check on Bob Rowe. She had almost decided that she would have to make her own decisions and forget about help from Brad when he suddenly appeared. She was in the English garden, a neglected magazine on the wicker settee beside her.

"There ought to be a law," he said, folding his long legs onto a nearby hassock.

Suddenly, for Anne, the whole afternoon brightened. She had not realized how much she missed the calls of this gangling neighbor of hers.

"A law about what?" she asked.

"A law about a blonde girl with

green eyes wearing a pink sun dress — or whatever — and looking good enough to eat! You make a most disturbing picture for a man who's been running like crazy around the art galleries of New York in a blistering heat wave."

"You can't give me a feeling of guilt," Anne said firmly. "I know they're having a heat wave in New York. I know I'm enjoying the cool breezes of the countryside and lolling around. But I'm not going to feel repentant. I feel good! What were you doing in New York?" she asked abruptly.

His father had cabled he was sending some special tiles from Holland, Brad told her, and he had had to make arrangements to receive the shipment. Their business was in lower Manhattan, but the warehouse was in the Bronx, and it was his responsibility to see that the delivery was made immediately to prevent possible breakage. Anne looked at him curiously. This was not the Charles Bradford who had walked with her in the woods, or the one who had given her a welcome to Glenbrook party. This was a serious businessman, quite sure of himself and of his own capabilities. Then again he changed.

"Enough of this nonsense!" he said, getting up. "Why do we talk about business on a beautiful afternoon like this? I came over to ask you to come to my place for a swim. Our pool is not as large as the one at the Park-Savoy, but it's not so crowded, either. Only two, as of the next hour!"

"You're very kind," Anne said at once. "As a matter of fact, I was hoping I'd get a chance to show off my new swim suit. I really shouldn't have spent all that money for it."

Brad gave a shout of laughter. "That's what I like about you, Anne Rowe Carter. You hit straight from the shoulder, and you tell the truth. Get into your glamour suit, and I'll wait for you. I walked over here, but you might as well drive us back. Even a short cut is a long walk on a day like this."

It was only fifteen minutes later that Anne rejoined him and they drove the short distance to the Bradford estate. Anne was startled; she had expected a pillared home, something like The Queen's Grant. Instead, it was a stone house which looked as if it would have been equally serene in a European setting.

The roofs were steeply slanted and were punctuated by four large chimneys. The gable windows of the second storey projected from the roofs like small boats putting out from an ocean liner. Clipped hedges marked the driveway, and Anne, trying to conceal how baffled she felt, carefully parked the car in front of the main door. As she stilled the motor, she turned to Brad, who was smiling broadly.

"You have a swimming pool?" she demanded. "This looks like a thatched cottage in Brittany, except that it isn't thatched. If you have a swimmin' hole, of course — "

Brad laughed at her. "Some of this

is part of the original house on The Queen's Grant. The gables were added later. We've kept it as close as we could to the original. I think you'll enjoy looking around inside."

"But the swimming pool?"

"It's out back. Come in."

Anne followed him into the house and stepped into another era. The ceilings were low, and the heavy beams were either polished or painted. A middle-aged woman presided over the kitchen, which had a polished brick floor. Although she was cooking on a modern electric stove, the huge, brick-faced fireplace dominated the room. She nodded pleasantly to Anne, but apparently she was used to those who came to see the seventeenth century home and volunteered no comments.

When Brad put on his swim trunks and led Anne outside, she was equally surprised. There was a modern, free-form swimming pool, painted blue and surrounded by a tiled walk dotted with beach chairs. It could have been a part of the grounds of a luxury hotel.

Anne tossed her terry robe onto one of the sun chairs and said sharply:

"Come clean, Brad. You show me a seventeenth century house with a twenty-first century swimming pool. You talk about boundary lines and about lawyers in Chicago. I'm rather lost. Which is *you*?"

Brad eased himself down on the edge of the pool and dangled his long legs in the water. He had been having a bit of fun with her, he admitted. But the facts were simple. This estate was only a summer place for his mother and father; they had an apartment in New York City, and of course their business was there. They traveled a great deal.

"You might say I pick up the pieces," Brad concluded. "I open this place in summer and close it in the autumn. The swimming pool was my own idea. The boundary lines — well, they're more or less a conversation piece. But the lawyer in Chicago — I'm serious about that. I think you need help."

"I'm sure I do," Anne sighed. "Do you plan to go to Chicago soon?"

"As soon as I can," Brad promised. "But unfortunately I have to wait for another shipment. In the meantime, is Bob Rowe giving you trouble?"

Anne told him that Bob had been a perfect guest. But she was still uneasy. Dr. Hewitt had told her he had information on the requirements for a state rest home, and he would talk them over with her at any time. But until Bob's claims were settled, they could scarcely plan anything constructive.

Anne came over to perch beside Brad on the rim of the pool and kick her toes idly back and forth in the water. She told him of Bob's idea about selling some of the furniture and bric-a-brac through his father's firm and was surprised to find he thought it a feasible idea.

"But only, of course, if you want to sell," he added. "And it will have to wait until we find out more about our boy, Bob. In the meantime — "

Brad's arm slid around her waist, and she found herself in an involuntary dive into the pool.

Anne came up sputtering, but Brad, with a few long, easy strokes, had already reached the other end of the pool. Anne started toward him, but he managed to elude her. She finally turned on her back and floated, watching the few fluffy clouds chase each other across a sunlit sky. Brad followed her example and located beside her.

"Happy?" he asked.

"Mmmm," said Anne. "I'm as lazy as one of those clouds up there, and I feel terribly guilty about it."

"Why should you feel guilty?"

"There's so much to be done," Anne explained. "All my life I've been a doer. Don't you think everyone is happier when he has a purpose in life, a reason for living, so to speak?"

"Of course," Brad agreed. "I won't argue that point. But there's no harm in a little vacation, in my opinion.

Hi, George!" He interrupted himself as a small wiry man came out of the house, carrying a tray on which a pitcher tinkled with ice cubes and there were two glasses.

"I thought you might like a glass of punch, sir," George said, putting the tray on the table. He took two large, fluffy towels he had draped over one arm and put them on the sun chairs.

"You thought right, as usual," Brad said cheerfully, as he swam over to the ladder and climbed out of the pool. "George helps me batch it while the folks are away. This is Miss Carter, our next door neighbor."

The servant acknowledged the introduction and went back into the house, and Anne dried herself off and leaned back on the webbing of the sun chair. She took a sip of the tall frosty drink and said appreciatively:

"Wonderful. Not too sweet. What is it?"

"George never gives out his recipes.

Frankly, I suspect he makes them up as he goes along." Brad fell silent, looking suddenly serious. "Not to change the subject," he said finally, "and not to change your mind about the rest home in any way, but how does your doctor friend fit into the picture?"

"What do you mean?" Anne asked.

"I mean, is he interested in having you start a rest home up here? Isn't he older than you are?"

"Steve is twenty-eight," Anne said shortly. "He is a surgeon, and a good one. He has his own practice — Park Avenue. He doesn't approve of the rest home in theory, but he does like it at The Queen's Grant. In fact, he had such a good time he's coming up to spend a few days as soon as he can get away. Does that tell you all you want to know?"

"No. What I want to know is, are you — is he — has he — ?"

"We're not engaged, if that's what you're trying to find out in a subtle, roundabout way."

148

"But he hopes to be. So he's coming up here to pin you down. And you've been leading him on . . . "

"You're going too far, Brad," said Anne, putting her glass on the table with a thump. "Steve and I are just good friends; nothing more."

"Methinks the lady doth protest too much," quoted Brad, smiling.

Anne was annoyed. "I don't see why you take it upon yourself to speculate on my love life," she said hotly. "Surely you must realize I had friends before I came to Glenbrook!"

"Uhh-huh," drawled Brad irritatingly. "How green your eyes are when you're angry!"

Brad was sitting forward in his chair, looking at Anne, his back to the house. As she saw two figures coming around the corner, Anne smiled with delight.

"Surely you must admit that there can be a firm friendship between a man and a woman, like the friendship between you and Cynthia Boynton, for instance?"

Brad scowled. But before he could answer, the debutante hailed them as she and Bob Rowe came toward the pool.

"Surprise!" she said in her husky voice. "I told Bob we'd find you dunking yourself in this water hole. Bob and I were going to swim in the pool at the hotel, but it was getting crowded. So here we are!"

Brad got up, gave Cindy his chair and shook hands with Bob. George appeared with a replenishment for the pitcher and two more glasses. The debutante looked at Anne appraisingly.

"Quite a bathing suit," she said insolently. "Do you do much swimming? I mean, have you time for it in addition to your duties as a nurse?" As she spoke, Cindy slipped out of her robe and revealed her own scarlet bikini.

"Even a nurse has some time of her own," Anne retorted.

"Me, I'm going to get cooled off," Bob interrupted, and dove into the pool.

"Hey, wait for me!" said Cindy, and made a clean, graceful dive into the water. As she might have expected, Anne thought with grudging admiration, the debutante was an accomplished swimmer; she apparently did everything well.

"Would you like to go in again?" Brad asked.

"No," Anne told him. "I have a slight headache, and I think I'll go back home."

"What are you two whispering about?" Cindy asked, coming out of the pool. "How about a glass of punch, Brad?"

"I was telling Brad I have to go back to the house," Anne said as she tied the belt of her terry robe.

"Don't let me drive you away," Cindy drawled.

"You couldn't," Anne assured her. She disliked the debutante more every time she met her, Anne thought. "No, don't bother coming around to the car," she told Brad. "And thank you for a delightful afternoon."

Cynthia put an arm around Brad's neck and started to dance. "Couldn't we have the record player out here?" she asked. "This tile makes a good dance floor."

"Tell Mrs. Stone I won't be in for dinner," Bob called after Anne. "A crowd of us are going over to the summer playhouse."

The nurse was feeling very sorry for herself as she drove the short distance to The Queen's Grant. It was odd, she reflected, how easily a person like Bob Rowe could fit into any group in spite of his lack of credentials. But a person like herself, with a profession and a real purpose in life, found it difficult to gain acceptance from those like Cynthia Boynton who thought of no one but themselves and did nothing they did not find amusing.

She went at once to her room and took off her suit and had a shower. Then, feeling better she dressed and went downstairs and out into the kitchen, intent on telling Mrs. Stone she would be the only one home for dinner.

As Anne pushed through the swinging door, she stopped in sudden shock. Cocky Biermann was sitting beside the table, one sleeve of a dirty, ragged shirt torn away and his arm dripping blood. Mary Stone, with a bowl of hot water, was dabbing at the ugly-looking gash, while Cocky was protesting in a high, reedy voice:

"'Tain't nothin', I tell you. Just a little cut. I was choppin' down the brush over on the boundary line, and the axe swung around and caught me. If the darn thing would just stop bleeding — "

"Oh, Miss Carter, I'm so glad you're home," Mary Stone said truthfully.

Cocky Biermann looked around and gave a toothless grin. He looked the same as he had that day in the woods, but now he was no longer frightening, but a hurt old man.

"Don't bother about me," he protested, trying to get up. "I'll just be runnin' along home now . . . "

Anne put a hand firmly on his shoulder. "You stay right where you are, Cocky. I'll go upstairs and get my first aid kit," she told Mrs. Stone, "and we'll see if we can get the cut cleaned up. When did it happen?"

"About an hour ago, I guess" Cocky said vaguely.

Anne flew upstairs for her kit, but paused long enough to put in a call for Dr. Hewitt. He was not at home, but she explained to the girl who answered what had happened and asked if the doctor could get a tetanus shot right away.

When she got back to the kitchen, Cocky eyed her suspiciously as she tore off the tattered remnants of his shirt and tried to clean up the cut. It was an ugly gash, and there was no doubt about the infection; Cocky obviously did not believe in baths.

"Will I call the doctor?" Mary Stone asked anxiously.

"I already have," Anne told her,

sponging away the blood and dirt.

"Now why'd you do that for?" whined Cocky. "I don't need no doctor stickin' me with needles."

"You'll have a doctor," Anne said, putting on the bandage.

"Don't believe in 'em," said Cocky vehemently. "I ain't goin' to see Hewitt — and you can't make me!"

10

ANNE, securing the bandage, asked abruptly: "Where do you live, Cocky?" It had occurred to her there might be another solution; Dr. Hewitt could go to the old man's house.

"I got me a little shack on the other side of town — about a mile up Greenwood Lane. It's a dirt road, but kept up good."

"Shack is right," Mary Stone said scornfully. "That place is going to fall down around your ears one of these days."

"You live alone?" Anne asked.

"For the last twenty years," Cocky boasted.

Anne shook her head. "You shouldn't be alone for a few days at least. There must be a boarding house . . . "

There was, the housekeeper said.

156

Myra Williams kept a nice, clean house, and she was a good cook. When Cocky protested he did not want to spend all that money, Anne offered to pay the bill. But she knew the old man liked his independence and had his mind stubbornly set on going back to his own place.

Mary Stone went upstairs and came back with a clean shirt for Cocky. It was one of Jim's and hung on the old man's scarecrow frame like a tent. But the faded blue denim was spotlessly clean, and Cocky seemed to sit straighter in the chair when he had it on. Anne improvised a sling out of a clean dish towel. This, too, he protested against until Anne explained that the quickest way to stop the bleeding was to keep the arm quiet.

"I'm sorry Jim ain't home," Mary Stone said, "but he went to that auction up to the Colton place. His ankle was bothering him a little bit, and I thought he ought to keep off it for a while."

"I'll run you down to the village,

Cocky," Anne promised. "Mrs. Stone can make you a strong cup of coffee while we're waiting . . . "

The telephone rang, and the housekeeper picked up the extension. "For you," she said, holding out the phone. She nodded as Anne silently asked a question, and Anne quickly went into the hall to speak on the phone there. It was Dr. Hewitt, and he had the anti-toxin shot ready.

"But we have a problem," Anne said ruefully. "Cocky doesn't want me to bring him to your office; he wants to go home."

"The old coot," Dr. Hewitt snorted. "He'll have gangrene sure in that shack. Did you tell him he might lose his arm?"

"I didn't want to frighten him," Anne explained. "He's lost quite a lot of blood. Mary Stone suggested he go to stay with Myra Williams for a few days, and I offered to pay the bill."

"Good idea!" Dr. Hewitt approved. "Myra Williams' place is just down the street from my office. I'll go down and wait for him inside. Think you can get him that far?"

"Of course," Anne promised as she hung up. Then she went back to the kitchen and discovered Cocky had taken advantage of the housekeeper and slipped out of the house while her back was turned. Anne ran to her car and set off in pursuit.

It was surprising how far the old man had managed to get in the very few minutes he had been out of the house. But when she saw him, he was slowing down and stumbling a little; Anne thought he was probably bewildered by this sudden weakness.

She stopped beside him and curtly ordered him into the car; Cocky looked as if he wanted to refuse, but Anne's determined expression and the ring of authority in her voice won out. The old man made one last effort to get her to drive to his home, but finally gave in and told her where Myra Williams lived.

As Anne brought the car to a halt before the neat white frame house, a stout middle-aged woman in a starched housedress came out onto the porch and advanced toward them. She nodded to Anne and opened the door on Cocky's side.

"Got yourself hurt, did you?" she said truculently. "Always knew you would, some day. Well, get in the house. I got your room all ready. Supper's five o'clock."

Myra Williams took Cocky by his good arm and almost lifted him out of the car.

"I have a message for you, Miss Carter," she said with a broad wink behind Cocky's back. "He asked if you'd go to his office and wait for him till he gets back from the hospital."

Anne interpreted this to mean the doctor was already at Myra Williams', especially when she saw the effect it had on Cocky. He straightened up and shook off the woman's arm.

"At the hospital, eh?" he chortled.

160

"Well, I don't mind stayin' with you a few days, Myra. It's kinda rough to cook for yourself one-handed. Supper at five? Tell the truth, I'm mighty hungry."

"I got a good beef stew and apple pie," Myra Williams said. "You could do with a little more meat on your bones, Cocky."

★ ★ ★

As Anne waited on the broad veranda of the doctor's home and office, she smiled as she thought of the scene taking place in one of the rooms in the Williams' home. She could just imagine Cocky's indignation when he found he had been tricked into getting 'a needle stuck into him'; it was only surprising his protests couldn't be heard this short distance away.

But then, Anne reflected, Dr. Hewitt probably had his own way of handling recalcitrant patients, especially those he had known most of their lives.

And Myra Williams looked capable of handling a man as small and thin as Cocky. She might lock him in his room if she had to, Anne thought. But probably, after one of Myra's hearty meals, he would be glad to stay on.

It was a little more than a half-hour later that Dr. Hewitt came walking up the street, carrying his bag. Anne went to meet him, and the silver-haired doctor greeted her with a conspirator's smile.

"Did he give you a hard time?" Anne asked.

"He tried to," Dr. Hewitt admitted, "but I've handled tougher patients than Cocky. I scared the living daylights out of him about gangrene. Lord knows it's bad enough, but I made it sound even a little worse. I even threw in lockjaw." He chuckled. "But he took the shot, and that's the main thing. I'll look in on him again tomorrow."

He invited Anne into his office, but agreed with her that it was pleasant on the porch and excused himself while

162

he took his bag into the house. When he came out again, he had taken off his jacket and was carrying a gray brochure.

"You have a copy of the regulations for a rest home," Anne said, her eyes sparkling. "Now we're really getting somewhere."

"I have a copy of the *new* regulations," Dr. Hewitt said gravely as he settled himself in a rocking chair beside hers. "I did not realize how many changes there had been. We'll have to discuss this rather carefully."

"Do you mean The Queen's Grant isn't suitable? Oh, Dr. Hewitt, surely no one could question that!"

"Let me show you what I mean," the doctor said. He took out his glasses, and put them on, then leafed through some of the pages. "For example, this: 'On or after the effective date of these regulations — '" he interrupted himself to say, "seven years ago — 'all buildings not previously licensed as rest homes shall be of new construction or of such construction that upon suitable alterations they will meet the standards established by the Department.' The Department of Public Health, that is."

"But surely we're all right, then! The Queen's Grant is a beautiful house, in excellent repair. Nothing is wrong . . . "

"My dear," Dr. Hewitt said kindly, "bear with me for a minute or two. Here's another regulation: 'Fire extinguishers shall be recharged and so labeled at least once a year.'"

"That's okay," Anne said brightly. "A fire extinguisher is not ornamental, but we could always place one behind a screen, or in a corner where it wouldn't be noticeable."

"Here's another," Dr. Hewitt went on. "'All exits shall be clearly identified by exit signs, adequately lighted, and shall be free from obstruction.'"

"Oh!" The thought of The Queen's Grant with exit signs over all the doors was definitely depressing.

"A few more requirements at

random," Dr. Hewitt went on relentlessly. "'All stairways used by boarders shall be well lighted and provided with hand rails on both sides.'" Anne thought of the lovely curved staircase at The Queen's Grant with its hand-turned outside rail and the scenic wallpaper that would be destroyed when another rail was put against the wall. "'Single rooms shall have one hundred square feet of floor area,'" Dr. Hewitt read. "'Multi-bed rooms shall have a minimum of seventy square feet of floor area per adult bed, with at least three feet between beds.'" He paused and looked at Anne over his glasses.

"In other words," Anne said gloomily, "I had a dream, and the sweet dream died."

"You're not giving up so easily, are you?" Dr. Hewitt demanded.

"Isn't that what you want me to do?"

"No, my dear," Dr. Hewitt sighed and took off his glasses. "But making dreams come true sometimes takes a little adjustment. You must realize that when you set up a rest home, you are making yourself responsible for other people's welfare — actually, for their lives. These regulations are established for their protection, and you must conform. But in the case of The Queen's Grant, there are other factors to be considered, too."

He was referring, of course, to the claim of Bob Rowe on the estate, the doctor explained. If structural changes were to be made in the house, it would be folly to start them unless Bob's claim was invalid or he agreed to cooperate.

Anne explained that Charles Bradford was going to help her with this, but he would have to go to Chicago and could not leave immediately. Dr. Hewitt agreed that Brad might be able to get some leads from a Chicago lawyer, but he still looked troubled, and Anne waited to hear what was disturbing him.

He said abruptly: "My dear, forgive

an old man for being so frank, but you must know you are very young and quite beautiful. I heard Dr. Steve Atkinson speak of you at Brad's party at the Park-Savoy, and I would guess that he has noted these facts. Whether or not he is the lucky man, it stands to reason you will be married and will have a family of your own. You will have many and varied interests; what will then become of the rest home?"

"I didn't intend to run it by myself, Dr. Hewitt," Anne said stiffly. "Of course I will hire an adequate staff . . . "

The doctor dismissed this with a shrug. "You can't be responsible for a set-up of this kind and have much of a private life. None of us can foresee the future, but at least one ought to look ahead before one takes a step as big as this one."

Anne's eyes clouded with tears, and it was a minute before she could speak. Even then, her voice was choked.

"I thought you liked the idea of

setting up a rest home at The Queen's Grant. I thought you were on my side."

"It is my dearest wish," Dr. Hewitt assured her. He leaned over and patted her hand. "I happen to know two other doctors — slightly decrepit, like myself — who have been thinking along the same lines. If we formed a sort of syndicate and worked with you, perhaps it would be better than having you alone responsible."

"But I would feel left out of it!"

"You wouldn't be. Only — and I say this from a pinnacle of advanced age — you shouldn't accept such a big responsibility. Look at it this way: your first guests would be from this area, within a radius of, say, fifty miles. The other two doctors and myself have contact with enough older people to fill The Queen's Grant overnight, so to speak. This way, each of your guests would have her or his own doctor on call. That's a regulation, too!"

"But my idea was so different," Anne

168

protested. "Why can't I do what I want to do in my own way? Why can't I open my home to those who need rest and shelter?"

"A lovely thought," Dr. Hewitt agreed. "Perhaps in another era, your idea would have worked. It may even work today. But I would be less than a friend if I tried to conceal the obstacles in your way. You see, dear girl, there is one factor you haven't taken into consideration."

Anne looked at him in surprise.

"I mean the factor of age. When you are dealing with children, they are predictable, in a way. The average, normal child of five, say, learns at a certain rate and develops skills at a certain time. But when you are dealing with people in a rest home, you have a number of different personalities. And I mean different! Is your mother living?"

"No," Anne faltered, "she died some years ago."

"But at the time she died, she had

a personality and traits of her own. They were formed because of her environment, her mode of living, her education. She was like no other person her own age. That's why those who live in a rest home, or any other institution, must be bound by rules and regulations. Otherwise they do as they please, and no communal effort can succeed that way."

Anne was stunned by his words. She felt as if her whole world had collapsed about her.

"Dr. Hewitt, I'm so discouraged I want to cry," she said finally. "Where do I go from here? Just sell off the place, as Bob Rowe suggested? Forget about the whole thing?"

"My dear girl," Dr. Hewitt protested, "maybe I've thrown these facts at you a little too fast. But please don't feel I've been deliberately discouraging you. Your idea was sound. It is a great thought, and you can bring many people happiness. But you have to walk before you can run."

"Meaning what?" Anne demanded.

"Meaning you have to settle Bob Rowe's claim first of all. Then, if you really want to set up a rest home at The Queen's Grant and plan for a medical advisory board, I'll be right in there cheering for you! The other problems we can take up as they occur. But, my dear, and I say this as a new friend, but a very devoted one, your own personal problems must be settled by yourself. Don't minimize them. You are entitled to a full and natural life; if you settle for anything less, you will be cheating yourself!"

After Anne had gone back home and was eating her solitary dinner, she was still a little depressed, but gradually she began to feel better. Dr. Hewitt had urged her to get Bob Rowe's claim straightened out first of all; this she was trying to do. Then he had felt she should plan for her own future. But this, she thought, was not an immediate problem, or one that concerned Dr. Hewitt particularly.

Maybe he was right; but on the other hand he could be wrong!

Mary Stone had greeted her with the news that a telegram had been telephoned to her: Dr. Atkinson would arrive on the weekend to stay for a few days if that was convenient. Anne sent a warm telegram of welcome in return. Maybe, while Steve was visiting, she could make up her mind about him.

"Myra Williams phoned me, too," Mary Stone said as she served the coffee. "And she gave me a good dressing-down. She said she wouldn't have Cocky sleep in one of her beds until he was washed, and she finally got one of her other boarders to give him a bath. That's Myra for you. Sometimes I think even her backbone is starched."

"You've just given me an idea," Anne said. "Perhaps I'll put a little starch in *my* backbone. I have a feeling I'm going to need it!"

11

STEVE was driving up. In a letter he sent following the telegram, he explained he had something he wanted to talk over with her. Anne could guess what it was.

Was she, she asked herself as she shampooed her hair and went out to dry it in the sun, making a mistake in not saying 'yes' to Dr. Steve Atkinson? Could she possibly be in love with him without knowing it? She liked him tremendously. They had an interest in medicine in common, and she respected his ability. Although he was six years older, it might merely mean he felt protective. Brad, of course, was less than a year older, and as for protectiveness — all he did was find fault with her!

Steve Atkinson was better-looking than Brad, she admitted to herself. Not bigger, though. Not so athletic-looking. On the other hand, Brad had a manner of authority that grew on one.

Anne grinned to herself as she fluffed her hair. Here she was comparing the two men as if she could have her choice! How conceited could she get? Actually, Charles Hamilton Bradford Third was nothing to her; nothing but a good, if unpredictable, neighbor.

As if she had conjured him out of the blue, Brad came into the garden and dropped into a long canvas chair beside the glass-topped table.

"Thought you might like to know," he said without preamble, "that the shipment I was waiting for came through and I'm off to Chicago tomorrow. But today is free. How about a sight-seeing expedition?"

"Where to?" Anne's question was purely rhetorical.

"A place I know in the mountains about seventy-five miles from here. Beautiful scenery all the way; the food is tops."

"That would take all day," Anne commented.

"Well, you've got a day to spare."

Anne shook her head. "I have to be here at two in the afternoon. Steve Atkinson is arriving about that time."

"Ah, the ardent suitor!"

"I wish you'd stop saying things like that! I've told you before that Steve is just a good friend."

"He would choose a weekend when I'm going to Chicago," Brad said grimly. "And, if I may remind you, I'm going in your interest. It must be nice for a girl to have two men jumping through hoops to please her. Do you enjoy this feeling of power?"

Anne did not think the question should be dignified by a reply. She took advantage of her shampoo to throw her hair over her face and massage the back of her head with her fingers. Brad, too, maintained a stony silence. Finally he observed:

"Despite the scintillating conversation around here, I'm afraid I'll have to tear myself away."

"*Must* you go?" Anne murmured.

Brad rose in one furious leap which upset the canvas chair. He stared at it balefully, evidently half of a mind to leave it lay.

"Don't kick it," Anne said sweetly, "when it's down."

Brad jerked the chair up on its legs, and it promptly folded. Grimly he pulled it into shape, watched it for a moment as if he expected it to spring at him, then strode away across the lawn without a backward glance.

"Goodbye!" Anne called after him. He did not answer.

Anne pushed her hair back and sat with an elbow on the table, her chin in her cupped hand.

Men! she was thinking. How could a girl figure them out? When you came to think of it, what a chance a girl took in agreeing to marry one of the strange creatures! Not that Charles Bradford had asked her. But he had reminded her that the Chicago trip was wholly

176

for her sake. Well, he had promised to help her, and it was only a small gesture he was making. Even if he was setting out in a bad mood, he was the one who had made the original offer!

★ ★ ★

When Steve arrived, Anne was glad to see him. He was tired, but seemed genuinely glad to be there; his manner was a pleasant contrast to the surly attitude Brad had displayed a few hours before.

"Maybe I'll change my mind about your rest home," he said wearily. "Right now, I'd like to be the first candidate."

"Trouble at the hospital?" Anne guessed.

"Yes," Steve admitted. "I operated on this man — he had to have part of his hip bone removed — and put in the metal part. He came through the operation without trouble; there was absolutely no indication of anything wrong."

"But it does take a long time to heal . . . "

"He was prepared for that. But we got him out of bed and into a wheel chair in a few days; there was nothing wrong!" Steve sounded exasperated.

"Was it a blood clot?" Anne asked sympathetically.

Steve nodded. "He was sitting in the chair, talking with another patient, and, all at once, he was gone."

Such things sometimes happened, Anne knew, but for some reason Steve seemed more concerned about the incident than usual. Perhaps it was just because he was tired and needed this vacation more than he knew. Anne resolved that she must try to take his mind off his work for the next few days; words of sympathy were useless.

"We will talk no more about your work," she decreed. "I'll have Jim Stone take your luggage upstairs, and you can freshen up. Then we'll just laze around this afternoon and plan your vacation. It's a wonderful feeling to be able to extend hospitality to others; I am grateful to Aunt Anne for that alone."

Steve was docile. When he rejoined her in the conservatory a while later, he already looked rested and refreshed. Anne took him on a short walk through the woods, which were peaceful and quiet. They were on their way back to the house when there was a blood-curdling scream, and Steve instinctively ducked. An arrow narrowly missed him and lay, still quivering, on the ground.

"What gives?" he demanded.

"Butch!" Anne called. "Come out here this instant! You know you're not to shoot at people!" For answer another arrow whizzed through the air, but this one was wide of its mark.

"Don't tell me you still have Indians up here," Steve said with a grin. "Shall we take to cover?"

"No, Butch has only two arrows," Anne explained. They waited on the path, and finally Butch emerged from the bushes. As usual, his face was streaked with dirt and his once clean pullover was dirty. He regarded them warily.

"Butch, you owe Dr. Atkinson an apology," Anne said sternly. "Do you know you almost hit him with the first arrow?"

"I did?" Butch asked in pleased surprise. "I'm gettin' almost as good as an Indian, ain't I?"

"Look, young fella," Steve said in a reasonable tone, "I didn't come up here to be shot at. Who are you, anyway?"

Anne explained Butch's relationship to the Stones and then insisted the youngster come back to the house with them and have his supper.

During dinner and afterward, Anne was pleased to see Steve was visibly relaxed. Part of his attitude, she knew, was due to Bob Rowe's presence. Bob had set out to be particularly charming, and he kept them amused and entertained with stories of his travels which, Anne discovered, had been quite extensive. By common, unspoken consent, they all skirted the subject of Bob's claim to the estate and Anne's intention of making it into a rest home.

Just before he excused himself, Bob said to Anne:

"I hope you don't mind, but I told Cindy Boynton that Steve was coming up. She suggested we could hire riding horses in the village and ride along one of the dirt roads, maybe take a picnic lunch. If you want to, that is."

"Sounds wonderful," Steve said at once. "How about it, Anne?"

She had no alternative but to agree. Still, she felt Bob Rowe was taking on privileges of a host which he had no right to assume. She said she would have Mary Stone prepare the picnic and they could plan their trip the next day.

"I hear Brad is off on a trip," Bob said lightly. "Will he be back, or shall we include him in the party?"

"He won't be back by tomorrow,

I'm sure," Anne said, and thought she detected relief in Bob's attitude. But he left the living room soon afterward, and she and Steve were alone.

Steve immediately began to take her to task for her attitude toward Bob. It was not as if she had anything tangible against the man, he pointed out. He could be her aunt's legitimate grandson. To Steve, his attitude and manner pointed to the probability that he was.

Anne was on the verge of telling him about Brad's trip to Chicago, but sternly repressed the impulse. If Bob had made such a good impression on Steve, there was little she could say to change his mind. She could change the subject, however, and she proceeded to tell Steve about Cocky Biermann and the ugly cut he had given himself.

Steve was interested, as she had known he would be. He was grinning as she told him how Dr. Hewitt had conspired with her to make Cocky take 'the needle,' and he shook his head over the old man's reluctance to protect himself against blood poisoning.

"It's a miracle to me that some of these old-timers haven't passed on long since," he commented. "They seem to enjoy fighting against every law of health and cleanliness, simply to prove they know better than the entire medical profession."

"At least we did our good deed for the day," Anne said. "And Dr. Hewitt tells me Cocky is doing just fine now."

Steve remembered meeting the doctor when he had been at the party for Anne, and regretted he had not had a chance to talk with him. He took it for granted Dr. Hewitt would not be in favor of turning The Queen's Grant into a rest home.

"But he *is* in favor of it," Anne said, crossing her fingers because she was shading the truth a little. "Dr. Hewitt even suggests I have a doctors' advisory board. He told me he knows two other doctors in this area who would be glad to serve."

Steve crossed the room suddenly and pulled her to her feet. His glance was tender as he held her in his arms.

"Your name shouldn't be Anne," he said lightly. "It should be 'Mary, Mary, quite contrary.' I really ought to spank you for being a stubborn little idiot, but I think I'll kiss you instead."

* * *

The next morning Cindy and Bob came cantering up the road, leading two other mounts. Anne and Steve were waiting with the two picnic baskets Mary Stone had packed.

"I'd better enjoy this picnic," Anne had told Steve earlier. "I haven't been riding in such a long time I may have to eat dinner standing up."

"I know what you mean," Steve said with feeling. "And I count on you not to keep us in the saddle too long."

"I'll do my best," Anne promised. But she felt that Cindy and Bob were really in charge of the outing.

184

As always, Cindy was perfectly dressed. Her fawn-colored jodhpurs were fitted to emphasize her beautiful legs; her scarlet blouse and matching jockey's cap made her a bright and challenging figure. Anne had to make do with a pair of blue jeans and a blue pullover with a turtle neck. She fished a lump of sugar out of her pocket and fed it to the sorrel mare who was to be her horse.

"You'll just have to put up with me," she whispered. "I know I don't look the part, and I'm not much of an equestrienne. But I like you, and I think we'll do all right."

Steve handed up one of the hampers to Bob, then leaned down and picked up the other after he was mounted.

"Showing off!" Cynthia teased. "Do you pick up a handkerchief with your teeth while hanging from the saddle with one foot?"

"You'll sing a different tune, my lady, when you get hungry and want the food in this hamper. By the way, has anyone picked out the road we're going to take?"

Cynthia had thought they would take one of the roads leading through the Bradford estate, she explained. They were well kept up, and there was a lake about an hour's ride away.

"But Brad isn't here," Anne said in a troubled tone. "I think we should ask before riding over his property."

"As you say, he isn't here," Cindy said, wheeling her horse around. "He and I have ridden over to the lake before. It isn't as if we were peasants, poaching on the property of the lord of the manor. Anyway, I told George we were riding over this morning, and he made no objection."

No matter what comment she made, Anne thought bitterly, Cindy managed to twist her words so that she seemed in the wrong. But it was a beautiful morning; the mare, who was named Lady, lived up to her title; and Anne could not help enjoying the ride, even though Cindy managed to pair off with

Steve and leave her to bring up the rear with Bob Rowe.

The road through the Bradford estate led past the house and swimming pool and then narrowed as it went into the woods. A wall of natural stone marked the boundary between the Bradford place and The Queen's Grant for some distance. Then it was replaced by barbed wire, curving in toward the road they were riding on. Anne judged that this must be the acreage in dispute.

Suddenly, as they came around a curve, they saw a house. The windows had long since been broken out, and the roof sagged, as if from the weight of years.

"Brad ought to tear that place down," Bob commented. "It's just an invitation to hoodlums."

"You might tell him how to manage the place," Anne said sarcastically.

But Cindy gave a sudden war whoop and sent her horse flying down the road. Steve gave an answering shout and pursued her, and Bob Rowe followed. Anne attempted to hold in Lady, but she was not to be left behind. Finally Anne gave her her head and careened after the others.

I know I'm going to regret this, Anne told herself as she raced through the lacy pattern of leaves made by the sun shining through the trees. But 'when in Rome, do as the Romans do.' This is Cindy's picnic, sure enough.

12

DURING the next three days, Anne had ample opportunity to make the same remark to herself. And she had to admit Cindy's ideas were good. They drove to a summer resort fifty miles away and rented two boats; Steve and Bob made a great show of fishing and finally came up with a catch so small they had to throw it back. Cindy discovered there was an auction in a nearby town, and while they didn't stay long and didn't buy anything, Anne enjoyed listening to the bidding and the auctioneer's remarks.

A middle-aged woman in front of Anne had made no bids until a large, old-fashioned loom was put up for sale. This was apparently the prize of the auction for her. There was a man standing on the other side of the lawn

189

who was just as eager.

"Fifteen dollars," the woman bid anxiously.

"Sixteen," said the man.

"Eighteen," said the woman in an attempt to make a closeout bid.

"Going — going — " the auctioneer intoned.

"Nineteen," the man called.

"Twenty," the woman said with spirit, but it seemed to Anne her voice quavered.

There was a pause, and Anne whispered to Steve, "I hope she gets it. She wants it so much!"

"Twenty-one!" The man's bid crackled through the air, and the woman's shoulders sagged. The auctioneer looked toward her inquiringly, but she shook her head.

"Sold to the gentleman on my right in the back," said the auctioneer, pounding with his gavel. "Next item."

The woman in front of Anne suddenly gave a convulsive sob. A neighbor patted her on the arm. "Never mind," she said sympathetically; "you'll find another one somewhere around."

"I wanted this one," said the woman in front of Anne.

"Then why didn't you bid twenty-two?" said her neighbor in an exasperated tone.

"Because I didn't *have* twenty-two dollars," sobbed the woman. "I got only twenty."

"I hate to see anyone so disappointed," Anne whispered to Steve. "When something is important to you, it's hard to let it go. Even if there is another loom, it won't be quite the same."

But Cindy was bored with the auction. She suggested they drive on for lunch to 'Robin Hood Inn,' where the waiters were dressed in medieval costume and every table had its own loaf of home-baked bread served on a cutting board and cut by the waiter with a sharp dagger. As with Cindy's other ideas, this proved to be a good one; they had an enjoyable time dancing to the small but good orchestra, and the food was excellent.

Anne had enlisted the aid of Mary Stone and her husband in preparing a barbecue. She purposely did not mention it earlier, but insisted they all drive back to The Queen's Grant when they left the Robin Hood Inn. She was resolved Cindy should not have everything her own way.

The barbecue had been set up in a corner of the English garden, and after dark Jim Stone provided special lights to ward off the insects. Mary Stone had baked potatoes and roasting ears of corn; Jim broiled the steaks as if he were a master chef. Even Cynthia gave grudging admiration to the menu and forgot her usual dainty manners as she bit into an ear of corn dripping with butter. Anne felt that at least she had, in a way, gotten even.

When the telephone rang after nine, she was prepared to hear from Brad.

There had been no word from him since he had gone to Chicago, and she was amazed at the way her heart fluttered when she thought he was calling. But Mary Stone, answering the ring, came back and reported the call was for Dr. Atkinson. Steve got up from his sun chair reluctantly.

"I knew it was too good to last," he grumbled as he went into the house. "A doctor's lot is not a happy one."

"One of the reasons I didn't marry you, darling," Cindy said pertly. She looked at Anne as she spoke, but Anne refused to comment. She knew the debutante was implying that Anne was Steve's second choice, but it seemed a petty point to discuss.

As they had expected, when Steve came out he told them it was a summons from New York. He would have to leave the first thing in the morning. Then he lapsed into silence, and it was clear he was waiting for Cindy and Bob to go. Cindy took the hint, and Anne, knowing she faced a showdown with Steve, went into the living room.

"I had hoped to have a little more time," Steve said gloomily, striding up and down the room. "But I guess it wasn't to be. Anne, I came here for a special purpose. I wanted to ask you to marry me and to give me my answer now. I don't think I've rushed you up to now. But this visit hasn't turned out the way I intended — we haven't had a minute alone."

"That's not my fault," Anne defended herself. "You know how Cindy takes over. And I thought you enjoyed our rural pastimes."

"I did. I'm not ungrateful. I've had a good time and a marvelous rest. But, Anne, you can't keep me dangling forever. You must have decided one way or the other. Won't you give me an answer now?"

"If I gave you an answer now, Steve, I'm afraid it would be 'no,'" Anne said as gently as she could. "You know I have my heart set on making

The Queen's Grant into a model rest home. You don't approve, and you would insist I give up the idea if I married you. I don't think this is a firm basis for marriage."

"But it's a silly idea!"

"It is not!"

"It is!"

"Oh, Steve," Anne protested, "why can't you let me have my way? Surely you must love me enough to let me have a little independence."

"But it's such a waste of time . . . "

"Not from my point of view. Marriage requires a certain amount of concession on both sides. If you can't let me make a decision before we're married, how can I hope to be anything but a slave afterward?"

"A woman is supposed to do as her husband wants her to."

"I'm not the 'patient Griselda' type," Anne said shortly. "Most women are not, in this day and age. We have minds of our own, and the right to live our own lives. You want to go back to the past, Steve, when a woman had to cater to a man in order to be supported."

"Sometimes I wish we were living back in the caveman era," Steve said bitterly. "I'd be glad to drag you off by the hair of your head and make you cook my venison pie. All right, So it's 'no' for now. But remember — you haven't heard the last of me."

★ ★ ★

When Steve had driven back to New York the next day, the house seemed suddenly very quiet. Of course Cynthia Boynton had turned her attention elsewhere, and Bob Rowe was around only at intervals. There were times when Anne was so lonesome she would have welcomed a chance to talk even with him. Dr. Hewitt had gone to Maine for a two weeks' vacation, and everything seemed at a standstill. There was still no word from Brad.

Anne was wondering about that a

few days later as she sat on the window seat in the library. The book she had begun to read was open on the cushion beside her; it could not hold her interest. Shadows were lengthening across the lawn, which did not look its best. Brown patches had begun to mar the green of the clipped grass as the dry spell had continued day after day in spite of repeated forecasts of rain.

"Lovely!" At the unexpected sound of Bob's voice, Anne jumped a little.

"Don't be frightened; it's only me," said Bob Rowe close behind her. His footsteps had made no sound on the thick rug.

"'I,' not 'me,'" said Anne, merely to have something disparaging to say.

"Tut-tut," Bob said, "what's grammar among cousins? Kissin' cousins, at that."

Anne instinctively drew back.

Bob laughed and sat on the window seat beside her. "Fear not. I won't kiss you until you agree to marry me. You yourself said we were second cousins," he said at her start of surprise. "We won't have feeble-minded children."

He picked up the book she had been reading and put it down with a mock shudder as he looked at the title. "New England in the 19th Century," he quoted. "No wonder you threw the book down and just stared out the window."

"I didn't throw it down," Anne said stiffly. "I was looking out the window because I thought I smelled smoke. I was wondering if there was a fire nearby."

"Oh, that!" Bob took the opportunity to edge nearer Anne on the window seat. "Cocky Biermann has recovered enough to get back to work and is now burning underbrush, dead grass and stuff. I told him not to set the place on fire. He's right over there by the boundary. It made him mad."

"I should think it would," Anne said, "Cocky doesn't own the place, but he feels a proprietary interest. I didn't know he was well enough to work again, however."

She turned and looked out the window again, and Bob, too, was silent. "Did you want something special?" she asked finally.

"Very special, my dear cousin. I came to ask you to marry me. Not right away," he interposed as Anne started to rise.

"You mentioned marriage before. Surely you're not serious!"

"Very serious, Anne. I don't require an answer right away, but I would like to get my name on your list of suitors. I gather Steve Atkinson didn't get very far with his courtship visit, so I should have a chance." Bob regarded her gravely, and Anne saw that he did indeed mean what he said.

"Perhaps, when I first came here, I antagonized you by sounding off against making this place into a rest home; the idea was new to me. But lately I have begun to reconsider. If we were married and ran the place together, it might work out. A rest home could be a real money-maker."

"That isn't the reason I want to start a rest home!" Anne flared.

"No, I didn't think it was," Bob said smoothly. "But somebody in the family has to be practical. You keep your ideals, and I'll look after the filthy lucre. We would make a good combination, a winning team."

Anne settled herself on the window seat again and looked at Bob scornfully. "It might interest you to know I wouldn't marry you if you were the last man on earth."

"Probably you wouldn't have a chance, *then*." Bob leaned back comfortably and crossed his legs. "In that case I'd have my choice of the world's lovelies, wouldn't I? Beauty pageant winners, Hollywood stars — darling, you'd be trampled in the rush, I shouldn't wonder. Not that you aren't a good-looking girl yourself," he added hastily. "And of course you have many added attractions. As a trained nurse, you'd be a decided asset around the house. Can you cook, too?"

In spite of herself, Anne laughed. "Now you're being silly."

"One of my many charms," said Bob Rowe. "One of my many charms, in addition to my attractive appearance, polished manners and sparkling dialogue, carried on at the moment with — if you'll excuse my saying so — very little encouragement from present company."

Anne turned back to the window and looked out again for a second without really seeing anything. Then she jumped to her feet.

"Look!" she cried excitedly. "The smoke's so thick now you can't see through it. We'd better see what happened to Cocky."

She ran for the door, Bob right behind her. As they neared the stone wall separating The Queen's Grant from the Bradfords', Cocky was beating futilely with a shovel at a patch of fire that had leaped the wall and was eating at the dried grass. In back of the old man, the fire was crackling toward a tangle of bushes on Brad's place.

Anne started toward Cocky, but Bob pulled her back. "We've got to find shovels or rakes if we want to help," he cried. "They're kept in the garage." She nodded, choking on the dense smoke, and they ran back over the lawn together.

By the time they had the tools, in only a matter of minutes, the fire had inched its way toward a clump of low-growing junipers on the lawn. Anne, armed with a long-handled shovel, stopped and beat at the blaze, while Bob ran on toward Cocky.

In another second Mary Stone ran out with a broom and slapped at the flames so valiantly it soon became apparent it was under control on that side of the wall. Meanwhile Bob was shouting something Anne could not understand. He was on the other side of the wall, using his shovel to throw loose dirt on the fire there. Finally, just as she understood he was yelling: "Send in the alarm!" Jim Stone came limping toward them, carrying a rake.

"I already phoned," Jim called in passing. "The engine's on its way; they saw the blaze from the fire tower."

"Not that it'll do much good," Mary Stone said, pausing to catch her breath. "We've got no big hose connection. But anyway, it will bring more men, and I think we've got it stopped for the moment on this side of the stone wall."

"We'd better watch awhile anyhow, just in case," Anne said, leaning on her shovel. The fire engine, its siren screaming, came up the road and turned into the Bradford place. Immediately behind it was a parade of vehicles, probably, Anne thought, members of the volunteer firemen's association, as well as interested spectators.

"I'm sure glad the fire is over at the Bradford place," Mary Stone said thankfully. "He has two wells; eventually they should be able to handle it."

"In a dry spell like this," Anne wondered, "why would Cocky try to burn the brush?"

"Because he's a stubborn old coot who thinks he knows better than anybody else," Mary Stone said acidly. "He knows he's supposed to get a burning permit, weather like this, but he just goes ahead and does as he pleases. Probably it would have been all right," the housekeeper conceded, "if his arm hadn't been hurt. So far as I know, Cocky never got in trouble before. But once he'd started the fire, he couldn't control it with one hand."

"I'm sorry for Cocky," Anne said. "But in a way, I'm even sorrier for Mr. Bradford. It will be hard for him to come home and find his property almost destroyed."

Mary Stone said nothing. Anne looked at her; she was gazing at the neighboring property where, she could see when the smoke was occasionally blown away, many figures were scrambling over the road and chopping at the bushes. The housekeeper, she remembered, did not care for Brad.

"Don't you feel sorry for him?" Anne persisted. "It's such a terrible thing to have your home burn down while you're away."

"He isn't away," Mary Stone said flatly. "He came home yesterday."

Anne felt suddenly depleted. She had counted so much on Brad's return; in a way, she had lived for it.

Yet Brad had come back yesterday and had not even called her!

13

BY nine o'clock at night the fire at Brad's was out of control. Truckloads of workers from surrounding farms had arrived — from the big potato farm some miles away; from a commercial blueberry farm nearby. Anne and Mary Stone carried pails of drinking water and plastic mugs to the stone wall, where they could be reached by the fire fighters. At intervals the men were forced back from the inferno the woods had become. But to Anne, her efforts and Mary's to provide some measure of relief for the small army of men with their soot-blackened faces and charred clothing seemed rather pathetic.

"They must be exhausted," Anne fretted to the housekeeper. "Couldn't we make sandwiches or something?"

Mary Stone shook her head. "Not

with what we've got in the house. There must be a hundred men over there."

When Anne was still desperately trying to think of some way they could help, a truck arrived from the Park-Savoy. It was loaded with cartons of sandwiches, gallons of thermos jugs with coffee and cases of soft drinks. Mary Stone and Anne took up their places at the stone wall and handed out the supplies to the men as they took turns snatching a few minutes to visit the impromptu refreshment bar.

Other supplies began coming in: from a motel down the highway; from a lunch room in Glenbrook; from another hotel in the mountains. Housewives began sending cookies and cakes; one woman sent a cold roasted chicken and another a pie. Anne sliced up the pie, getting as many pieces as she could out of it, and tore apart a carton to make paper plates.

And still the fire made headway, now stealthily eating through underbrush toward the edge of the woods bordering on a summer cabin community. The fire fighters concentrated their efforts toward heading off the creeping flames in this direction, trying to turn them toward the corner where the woods thinned to almost nothing.

The abandoned two-storey house on Brad's property, which Anne remembered passing when they had started on their ride, escaped the fire for quite a while. But then a lively breeze sprang up, whirling burning leaves and bits of bark into the air; they caught high into the top of a half dead, tinder-dry old cedar tree near the house. It burst into flame, caught the top of a second tree and then a third.

"A crown fire!" muttered one of a little knot of men near this point. "We have nothing to fight this kind of a forest fire."

The flames were now leaping with malicious swiftness from tree to tree, shooting sparks as they went. Luckily there was a break here in the ranks

208

of trees which cut off a triangular wedge from the rest of the woods. The burning treetops were far enough away from the main area to keep the fire close to the ground the rest of the way.

Anne, like the other watchers flocking to the scene from the village and nearby communities, was relieved to see that the blazing treetops appeared to be burning themselves out with little danger of 'crowning' other trees.

But a second later there was a shout of dismay from the crowd. A burning piece of branch had whirled through the air and landed on the roof of the abandoned house, where scattered shingles, dry and crumbling, still remained. Instantly flames darted in a half-dozen directions at once, with flaming bits dropping through the great holes in the roof into the rooms below.

"There's a child in there!" someone screamed. "Look! Look! There's a child in there!"

Anne felt suddenly sick. When she had mentioned the house to Mary Stone earlier in the week, the housekeeper had told her the place was a favorite playhouse for children, although she had threatened Butch with dire consequences if she ever caught him near the place.

Now Anne was caught in the concerted rush of people toward the house, where, she saw with horror, there actually *was* a small figure outlined in the light of the fire. It seemed to be in a room just beyond where the burning shingles had fallen. Almost before the first gasp of horror had died away, a huge branch fell from a blazing tree and landed on the rotten wooden steps leading to the front door. The flames leaped high and effectively blocked the entrance.

Women hid their faces; two men who tried to leap past the flaming barrier were driven back; another crawled through a window and tried to reach the stairway, but it was already on fire. Others ran toward the back of the house. The crash of the back door was heard as they made their way into the kitchen. But in the newly created draft, the flames leaped higher and raced unchecked through the first floor.

A flimsy veranda ran along one side of the house. All that remained of its roof were the bare cross-timbers, and even these had caught fire at one point. The uprights that had supported the roof were slender, but now a man could be seen clambering swiftly upward in one of them. He was halfway up when one of the corner posts gave way and the skeleton porch roof on that side sagged almost to the ground.

"That's Bradford — Charles Bradford!" a woman screamed, and Anne's heart skipped a beat. Smoke was now pouring densely out of the window of the room where the small figure had been seen.

"The child is already overcome with smoke, or he would at least have reached the window," a man muttered.

When he voiced the thought, Anne

almost screamed, as many of the other women were doing. She watched Brad reach the timbers of the porch roof, saw one break as he tested it with his foot, silently prayed as he leaped lightly to the window sill and vanished into the smoke.

Meanwhile several men had gathered below the window, waiting and apparently hoping against hope that Brad would reappear with the child in his arms. Minutes went by; Anne's heart was in her throat as she wondered if Brad had been overcome by smoke and was lying up there unconscious.

But suddenly he was back, dimly seen in the swirling smoke and holding something in his arms.

"Catch!" he shouted hoarsely to the men below, and threw the figure toward the knot of men. Willing hands reached up to catch it and then retreated as Brad yelled, "Look out below!"

Brad took a couple of running steps along the beam and the next moment leaped to the ground, where he rolled over once or twice and came up grinning.

The object which the waiting men had caught was an old dressmaker's dummy. It had been cut off at the waist so that, standing on the floor, it had seemed to be the figure of a child. "No one is there!" Brad shouted to them. His face was streaked with soot, his shirt was gone — apparently he had torn it off when it had caught fire — and he was holding one hand as if it were hurt.

But he did not pause; he ran on to the next danger spot, and Anne and Mary Stone returned to the house.

By midnight the fighters had the fire under control. A handful of men were detailed to watch for a couple of hours with the understanding that their place would be taken by another group when their tour of duty was over.

Bob Rowe returned with this news; Anne, the Stones and Butch were in the kitchen devouring bacon and eggs and drinking scalding cups of coffee. Jim

Stone had been telling stories of former fires which had, in some cases, done considerable damage in the community. Young Butch, so excited at first he had almost been out of control, had been firmly held inside by his grandmother and at last had succumbed and fallen asleep over his glass of milk. Jim Stone carried him off to bed, and Mary soon followed them upstairs.

The trucks and the cars had left the Bradford place; the night seemed unusually silent after the shouts and cries that had rung through the air for hours. But the smell of fire lingered on.

"Lucky the fire didn't reach this house," said Anne her voice trembling a little.

"If the wind had shifted it might easily have caught," said Bob. "And with only the local fire-fighting apparatus, it might have been difficult to control."

"I was fortunate," Anne said.

"Depends on how you look at it," Bob Rowe said casually. "I know

Grandmother Rowe carried heavy insurance. It might have been the best thing for all concerned."

Anne refused to comment. She said only: "That was a brave thing Brad did to go into the burning building when he thought there was a child trapped there. He might have been killed."

"As I told you," Bob said, frowning, "Brad should have had the house torn down. He made a fine heroic gesture, but if he had had a little foresight, it wouldn't have been necessary."

"Will you turn out the lights, please?" Anne said, getting up abruptly. "I am weary."

"I'll lock up," Bob said shortly. "But I wish you would realize, Anne, that Charles Hamilton Bradford Third is concerned with only one person — himself!"

★ ★ ★

Brad came striding across the lawn the next morning with a purposeful air.

Anne's heart skipped a beat as she caught sign of his gangling figure, but she steeled herself against any show of emotion. If he could come back from Chicago and not call her when he knew how concerned she was about his trip there, probably Bob was right: he thought only of himself. She could take refuge in her pride and not let him know how deeply she was hurt.

Anne talked herself into what she considered a composed attitude by the time Brad came into the English garden. Then she saw the bandage on his hand.

"Oh, Brad, you're hurt!"

"Just a slight burn. Dr. Hewitt fixed me up."

"Well — " Anne felt rebuffed. "Anyhow, it was a brave thing you did."

"It was my property." Brad shrugged. He closed the subject and looked around sharply. "Where's Bob Rowe?"

"He had a date with Cynthia Boynton, I believe."

"Good!" Brad said in a businesslike manner. "I want to explain this without interruption. Jerry Linden, this lawyer I know in Chicago, and I had quite a session on Robert Lowe. It's an interesting story."

"When you didn't get in touch with me after you returned," said Anne stiffly, "I thought your trip had been wasted."

Brad looked at her sharply and then smiled. "Now don't get your back up!" he advised. "I wanted this to be a package deal, and there was someone I had to see first."

"But you could at least have let me know."

"Do you want to listen to me or not?"

"I'll listen," Anne agreed, "but I don't know why you have to be so mysterious."

Brad looked at her sternly. He began to talk, and gradually his manner softened. Anne sat listening with ever-increasing excitement as he unfolded the story of Bob Rowe.

Robert Roe was his real name, Jerry Linden had discovered, without the 'w'. He had been born in Chicago; not in Mexico. For a little over a year he had been hired as a bodyguard for a badly crippled millionaire and had traveled with him all through Europe. Possibly during that time he had met Anne Rowe, or at least come to know of her. Perhaps the idea of posing as her grandson had occurred to him then.

At any rate, the millionaire had died during one of his trips, and when Bob Roe returned to Chicago he found himself in difficulties. His travels and high living had given him a taste for the best; he could not settle down to an ordinary job. For a while he had stayed out of trouble, but then an elderly woman had complained she had been swindled out of two thousand dollars. Jerry Linden looked up the court record; to avoid scandal, the woman's family had not prosecuted.

Later on, the record showed, Bob

218

Roe was involved in minor thefts but had been convicted only once. He had served three months.

"I knew he was a phony!" Anne felt triumphant. "And I'm deeply grateful to your friend for finding out the facts. But what happens now?"

"That's the reason I didn't get in touch with you right away," Brad said in a hurt tone. "You may have thought I should have, but there was something else I had to do first. There's no use dragging this through the courts, and I think Bob would be happy if he thought it could be settled in an informal hearing. Jerry advised me to have you both appear before Judge Hilary Justin. He has a summer place in Leebrook, about thirty-five miles away. I saw him yesterday and gave him the photostats. He agreed to scare the living daylights out of Bob Roe!"

"Brad, how can I ever thank you?" Anne stammered. "I could never have done this alone."

He accepted the compliment with

a satisfied grin. "No, I don't think it would have been possible. Bob is a slippery customer. But of course I was glad to help. Now about these 'proofs' he is supposed to have: what are they?"

"So far as I know, they are the Mexican birth certificate, the letter from his mother, and the ring Aunt Anne is wearing in the painting."

"Is the ring genuine?"

"I'm not sure, but it seems to be."

"Probably he stole it; you told me your aunt died in Chicago." Anne nodded. "Well, if he did see her — and he probably did — he would have had a chance to slip the ring in his pocket. Now you have to get Bob to agree to put his claim before Judge Justin. Do you want me to go with you?"

Anne thought for a few seconds. "Maybe it would be better if I went with him alone. Bob doesn't like you."

"I know he doesn't. And Bob might smell trouble and try to get out of the hearing. Definitely, the man should not be in the house, and much as I would enjoy throwing him out personally, I think this is the better way."

"What will I say about Judge Justin?"

"Could you say someone in New York suggested him?" Anne nodded, and Brad rose to leave. "Then we've settled as much as we can for now," he added. "Don't let Bob suspect you have the evidence on him."

"He won't suspect," Anne said confidently. "As a matter of fact, he's so sure of himself he asked me to marry him a few days ago!"

"The devil he did!"

"I didn't accept," Anne assured him. "But he did make me an attractive offer: he said he would be glad to join me in setting up a rest home, and he thought we could make a lot of money."

Brad glared at her for a moment, then turned on his heel and stomped away.

14

BOB himself gave Anne the opportunity she had been waiting for. He returned from his date with Cindy Boynton in a bad mood, and Anne surmised the debutante was tiring of him as a companion. After dinner, he asked if Anne would come into the living room with him, and there he produced a sheaf of papers which he had had typed in the village.

"This is the inventory," Bob explained. "I've checked those items I think are particularly valuable and have no place in a rest home. By the way, did you ask Bradford if his firm would be interested in them?"

"Yes, I did. And he said they would."

"Then why don't we get this thing organized?" Bob asked. "I can't hang around all summer without knowing where I stand. Yet you won't even look at my proofs . . . "

"You are under no obligation to stay here," Anne pointed out. "But I agree it is a nerve-wracking situation. However, it would do no good for me to look at 'proofs'; I don't know the first thing about them. I would want legal advice. If you don't want to wait until fall and present what you have in court, I'd suggest we consult someone and get an informal hearing."

"Now you're talking," Bob approved. "Do you have any particular lawyer in mind?"

Anne told him about Judge Hilary Justin, in Leebrook, who had been recommended by one of her friends. She had not met the judge, she was careful to say, but she understood he had had some experience in dealing with settlements of estates.

Bob beamed his approval. There was no doubt he was sure of his ability to convince the judge that his claim was valid, but he questioned Anne closely as to whether or not she would abide by the judge's opinion. She thought it the better part of discretion to appear a little reluctant, but she admitted the judge had been highly recommended and surely knew the law. They agreed she would phone and request a hearing as soon as possible. Then, although Bob would have been glad to sit around talking, Anne pleaded a headache and went to her room.

It was two days before the meeting was arranged, and the day set was a dreary, rainy one. Brad had not been in touch with her and Anne did not know if he even knew the date had been set. She felt very much alone as she and Bob set out for Leebrook at eleven o'clock. He said he knew where the town was and offered to drive. Anne could foresee difficulties on the return journey, but she could think of no reasonable way to refuse.

"Why so pensive?" Bob demanded. "You look as mournful as if I were trying to do you out of everything.

There's enough in the estate for both of us, you know."

"I guess it's just the weather," Anne said. "Such a gloomy day!"

"Never mind. By this afternoon we should have the question settled, and then we can plan for the future. It can be a bright one, Anne, if we work together."

Judge Hilary Justin's home was a plain white house, but beautifully kept and with a colorful garden at one side. The judge himself opened the door as they came up the porch. He was a small, wiry man with sparse gray hair combed over a bald spot, and he was dressed in a casual sports shirt and slacks. Anne could see that Bob felt the man was unimportant and anticipated an easy decision; she was not too sure Judge Justin was capable of helping her.

He led them into what he called his 'library' — a large room with a big bay window, a few bookcases and a desk. Anne introduced herself and

Bob, and the judge sat behind the desk and invited them to take chairs facing him.

"I understand, Miss Carter," the judge said, "you were left some property by your aunt — " he opened a folder on the desk — "and that you, sir — " he looked sharply at Bob — "claim to be the natural grandson and want a part of that estate."

"That's it in a nutshell," said Bob smartly.

Judge Justin looked at him for a second and then said: "This is an informal hearing, but I'm not *that* informal."

"Excuse me," Bob muttered.

"Now, shall we let the lady speak first?" Judge Justin asked.

Anne began to outline the details of her aunt's will, as they had been reported to her, and described The Queen's Grant. She told the judge about her aunt's son, but said she had not known he was married, and there was no mention of it in the will. She started to tell the judge about her plans for a rest home, but he silenced her.

"My dear, there is an old French rule for court procedure: 'Stick to your mutton.' Your disposition of the property is not a part of this hearing. I think it is time we heard from your companion. How do you enter into this, sir?"

Bob produced his box and took out the birth certificate. When he laid it on the desk, the judge asked Anne: "Have you seen this?"

Anne admitted she had not. When she glanced at it, she smiled. "It's in Spanish; I wouldn't know what it said."

"I do know Spanish," said Judge Justin. "But of course this town no longer exists."

"That's right," Bob agreed. "It was wiped out in an earthquake."

Bob next produced the letter written by his mother; the judge barely glanced at it. "Is this all?" he demanded.

"No," Bob said, plainly annoyed at the judge's attitude. "I have this ring, given to me by my grandmother just before she had a fatal heart attack in Chicago."

To Anne's astonishment, he produced snapshots of the portrait of Aunt Anne which hung in the living room, with a closeup of the hand wearing the ring. He had not told her he was taking the pictures, but he evidently considered them his trump cards.

Judge Justin looked at the photographs and then examined the ring closely. "It looks like the same one," he said finally. Bob relaxed.

"It *is* the same. It's my grandmother's ring."

"Really?" It was only one word, but for Anne the room was suddenly changed. Now it was Judge Hilary Justin who sat tall in the chair and was the commanding figure. Bob seemed to shrink and lose all personality. Judge Justin again referred to the folder on his desk. Anne forgot about his sports shirt and slacks; if he had been wearing a white wig, as in the English courts, and a formal black gown, the judge could not have been more impressive.

"Young man," he said sternly, "in this folder I have a photostatic copy of your birth certificate. You were not born in Mexico, but in the charity ward of a Chicago hospital. Your mother was Lisa Roe — R-O-E — no 'w'. Your father was unknown."

"Now just a minute!" Bob shouted excitedly. "I don't know whose record you've got there, but it isn't mine."

The judge went on as if he hadn't spoken: "This is the birth certificate you used to obtain a passport to travel abroad, and that is the name you used until a few months ago. I also have a photostatic copy of your court record; you were convicted of theft and served three months. Your fingerprints are part of that record."

Bob sat as if turned to stone, his face a dull brick-red.

"If Miss Carter wants to prefer charges against you for attempted fraud — "

"Oh, no! I couldn't do that!" Anne exclaimed.

"That is your decision," Judge Justin conceded. "But I strongly advise you against further association with this man. He has been proved a thief and a liar."

Bob Roe suddenly sprang to his feet, snatched his 'proofs' from the desk and stalked out of the room. They heard the front door slam as he left.

Judge Justin smiled at Anne genially. "I guess we upset his apple-cart," he said with satisfaction. "Charles Bradford did a bang-up job on collecting the evidence I needed; he should have chosen law as a career."

Anne stood up and held out her hand. "You've been very kind, Judge Justin, and I do thank you for your time and trouble. But I guess I'd better be going along now . . . " She stopped in dismay. Bob had driven her to Leebrook, and he was already gone!

"I've arranged for you to get home

safely," the judge said smiling. He raised his voice slightly. "It's okay to come out now."

The door to an adjoining room opened, and Brad came in. "Are you all right, Anne?" he asked anxiously.

"Yes," she started to say. And then, without warning, the nervous tension of the past hours took its toll and she began to cry. Brad took her in his arms tenderly, and she sobbed against his shoulder.

"I don't know what got into me . . . "

"Never mind, never mind," Brad murmured; "cry it out. You've had a rough time, but it's all over now."

★ ★ ★

After Anne had thanked the judge again and they had left his home, Brad revealed that he was taking the long way back to The Queen's Grant. There was a small hotel not far away which had a dining room overlooking a quiet lake. He explained that they would have lunch there; he had already reserved a table.

As if to make up for the miserable morning, the skies had cleared and the sun was shining brightly. As they drove along a back road bordered with pines, the fragrance was heady and relaxing.

Anne sniffed the air gratefully. "Do you know," she said, "I actually feel hungry? Now that it's all over, I realize how much of a strain it has been. You were wonderful, Brad, to go to all this trouble for me."

"It was no trouble," Brad assured her, "and it's a pleasure to take you to lunch, although I do have an ulterior motive."

"An ulterior motive?"

"Yes. I want to give that crook a chance to pack up and get out of your home. You shouldn't have to see him again. I wonder why you didn't want to press charges."

She had been thinking, Anne said, that for all his debonair manner, Bob

Roe had really had an unhappy life. His ideas were twisted, of course, and sooner or later, unless he realized happiness was not something life owed a person, but something which had to be earned, he would discover he had wrecked his life beyond recall.

Brad argued that, in refusing to press charges, she had turned a known criminal loose. Bob would be free to continue his swindles or thefts until he was caught, but in the meantime innocent people would suffer.

"When you consider justice," Brad concluded, "you can't think of the criminal alone; you must consider society as a whole."

"Justice should be tempered with mercy," Anne reminded him. "What good would it do to lock up a young man who might make something of himself? Anyhow, I think Bob has definitely decided to reform."

"If everybody reasoned the way you do, we wouldn't need any jails at all," Brad retorted.

"You're exaggerating," Anne said. "And you seem determined to condemn Bob to a life of crime forever. Men have been known to change."

"Perhaps you're right," Brad said gently. "But while we're on the subject, what happened to your aunt's ring? I'm assuming it is genuine and that Bob, running true to form, stole it from her when she was in Chicago. It must be quite valuable, and it is surely yours. Did Bob hand it over to you?"

Anne flushed. Until Brad had reminded her, she had completely forgotten the ring. Now she remembered Bob had scooped up his 'proofs,' including the ring, before he slammed out of the judge's house.

"Well, you've answered the question," Brad said coolly. "I don't think it speaks well for your theory concerning Bob's reformation. He'll probably pawn it for get-away money."

"Bob always seemed to have enough money," Anne objected. "At least he never mentioned it, and although he didn't have many expenses, there were some."

Brad had a theory about that, too. He thought probably Cynthia Boynton had given Bob enough pocket money to escort her where she wanted to go. Anne was shocked at the thought, but Brad seemed sure of himself. And, knowing Bob's real background, she now realized he must have obtained money in some way. It also explained why he had been so anxious to sell off some of the furniture, even if she refused to sell the house.

They arrived at the hotel even as Brad spoke, and it was, as he had said, a pleasant place to be. They were shown to a table near the window overlooking the lake, and Brad refused to let her see the menu. The waiter set up mugs of hot clam broth before them, and as Anne sat sipping it and looking out over the water, she decided to forget Bob once and for all. The price of a valuable ring seemed a small one to pay for peace of mind.

A little later, the waiter tied bibs around their necks and then served them with perfectly broiled lobsters, French fried potatoes and coleslaw. Anne regarded the silver bowl of melted butter and looked at Brad accusingly.

"You want me to lose my figure."

"On the contrary, I think you're on the skinny side. Wouldn't hurt you to eat a little more."

"Aren't you flattering!"

"You get enough flattery from Steve Atkinson. I'm going to fatten you up. Don't let the lobster get cold."

Later, when Anne had sternly refused Boston cream pie, they lingered over their coffee. Brad told her about his parents and something of the export-import business. Then abruptly he switched the subject back to her future and what she was going to do with The Queen's Grant.

Anne didn't mean to, but she found herself telling him about her last interview with Dr. Hewitt and the many new regulations regarding such a home. She mentioned the exit signs, the fire extinguishers and the floor space required.

"I can see why Dr. Hewitt suggested a medical advisory board," Brad said thoughtfully. "It stands to reason that any business you start in this day and age is bound to be complicated."

"I'm not giving up the idea," Anne said stubbornly.

"What about when you get married?" Brad demanded. "Do you plan to commute between New York and The Queen's Grant?"

"Meaning am I going to marry Steve Atkinson? I haven't decided yet."

"Suppose you marry someone else? What man is going to stay tied down in one place when he has a young and beautiful bride he wants to show off to the world?"

"You can ask the questions," Anne said coldly, "but I'm not bound to give answers, even if I know them."

Brad shrugged. "I guess you have answered me," he said, signaling to the waiter for a check. "Let's get out of here. The luncheon party seems to be over."

15

IT was after three when Anne returned to The Queen's Grant, and Bob Roe had already gone. Mary Stone told her he had packed his luggage and left inside of a half-hour, with no explanation beyond the fact that she would hear the details later. She looked inquiringly at Anne.

"He was not Aunt Anne's grandson," Anne explained. "He was only trying to get his hands on some money from this estate. I'm afraid he is a thief and a swindler, Mrs. Stone."

The housekeeper looked shocked. "He was such a nice young man," she protested. "Never a cross word out of him, and so kind to Butch and all. I can't believe it."

The housekeeper's eyes filled with tears. "There's to be just you for dinner, then. I had thought to have steak . . ."

"No, Mary. A sandwich and a cup of tea will be fine. And I'll eat in the breakfast room."

At least, Anne reflected as she went upstairs, she could now give the orders in her own house. But the place did seem empty. Perhaps there was something to be said for Mary Stone's point of view. It didn't matter if a man was a thief, if he was never cross and had good manners!

Anne spent the next few hours trying to think things through. Her talk with Brad at lunch had been disturbing, but in a way it had clarified her position for her, at least as far as Dr. Steve Atkinson was concerned. He was not the type of man to allow her to keep The Queen's Grant if they were married. No matter what he promised her, Steve would get impatient and angry as the difficulties of the situation became apparent.

She was, in effect, telling herself she did not love Steve enough to marry him, Anne reflected. She must have known it before, but she had not been willing to admit it. Now she would have to acknowledge the fact and plan for her future accordingly. And since she was being honest with herself, Anne thought, she might as well go the whole way.

She was in love with Brad, but he thought of her only as a girl who did not know what she was doing. He had been kind and helpful, but probably he would marry Cynthia Boynton or someone like her. What had he said? 'What man is going to stay tied down in one place when he has a young and beautiful bride he wants to show off to the world.' Well, at least he had been candid.

That night, Mary Stone fretted as she set the breakfast table with a chicken sandwich, tea and a dish of fruit. "You'll get sick if you don't eat right," she remarked, and then apparently remembered Anne was a nurse. "But you know that as well as I do. And you do look tired," she added.

"I *am* tired," Anne agreed. "I'm tired far into the future. It's been quite a day. After I've finished, I'm going right upstairs to bed, so you needn't bother about me again until morning."

Still the housekeeper lingered. "What will that nice young man do now, Miss Carter? Has he got a job?"

"I don't believe so, but I don't know," Anne said.

"I miss him," the housekeeper said as she went out. "And so do Butch and Jim."

Anne followed her schedule, but once she had undressed and gotten into bed, it was maddening to find she could not sleep. After trying unsuccessfully for some time, she got up, put on a robe and went down to the library to get a book. None of the titles appealed to her, but she finally picked out five, brought them upstairs and dumped them on the bed. Then she climbed back into bed herself, leaned back against the piled-up pillows and began to read. She turned restlessly from book to book, finding it difficult to concentrate on any one. When she fell asleep presently, her light was still on.

She awoke after a while with the sense of someone staring at her. As her eyes flew open, they met those of Bob Roe standing beside the bed.

"Sleeping Beauty!" His voice was only a whisper. "Your prince has come to carry you off."

"How did you get in here?" demanded Anne loudly.

"Quiet!" said Bob with a finger against her lips. "You'll wake the Stones."

"But how — ?" Anne persisted.

"Through your door. It wasn't locked, you know. And if it matters, by way of one of the french windows below. I know this house as well as you do, remember."

"I thought you were on your way to Chicago."

"Without you? No, darling. I wouldn't desert you. Besides, I've changed my mind; I think Mexico would be better.

I've always wanted to see the place where I was supposed to be born."

"You're out of your mind," Anne retorted. "What gave you the idea I'd go to Mexico with you?"

"Because you love me," Bob said smugly. "And you did refuse to prosecute . . . "

"I was only trying to help you to — "

"Rehabilitate myself?" Bob grinned at her. "That's what you thought, but I know a woman never tries to make a man over unless she's in love with him."

"Will you get out of my room?"

"No."

"But how can I get up and dress?"

"Well, maybe it would be better," Bob conceded. "You'll certainly have to dress, since you're coming to Mexico with me. We can get a plane from Boston around dawn; I asked. That doesn't leave us too much time. All right. I'll go outside in the hall and wait for you. But I'll be right outside the door. Don't try to get away; don't try to telephone."

"Kidnapping is a serious offense."

"I'm not kidnapping you, darling. I'm persuading you to come with me. We can be married whenever it's convenient. Oh, I almost forgot! Here's your engagement ring."

He took out of his pocket Aunt Anne's topaz and diamond ring. Before Anne could object, he had caught her left hand, where it lay on the coverlet, and slipped the ring on her third finger.

"Allow me," he said, and stooped to kiss the ring in place.

"You didn't pawn it!" Anne said before she thought. "How are you going to pay for the plane tickets?"

"Never mind — I have money. Now get dressed."

Bob left the room, and Anne had slipped out of bed and was feeling for her slippers with her toes when the door opened again and he stuck his head in.

"Just bring an overnight bag. We'll

buy what you need in Mexico," he advised, and shut the door again.

Anne felt as if she were living through a nightmare, but she began to dress quickly. She would go along to the airport with Bob; surely there must be some way she could attract the attention of the police before she actually got on the plane.

Why was Bob Roe doing this to her? she wondered. He didn't love her; she had long discounted that possibility. And he couldn't force her to marry him. Was it all a joke? But what a mean joke, when she had only tried to help him!

It flashed through her mind that Bob might be a drug addict, although he had given no indication of it in the weeks she had known him. It would explain his wild idea of getting her to marry him to finance a costly drug habit.

Yet she had no money but what she had earned as a nurse — except for Aunt Anne's legacy. Perhaps Bob was counting on that!

Utterly confused, Anne pulled on a sweater and skirt and slipped into moccasins, threw a light topcoat over her shoulders and picked up her handbag. She took her overnight case from the closet and put in the books to give it weight, then stuffed in a towel to keep them from sliding around.

She saw the glitter of the diamond and topaz ring as she did so and wondered momentarily if she dared take it off and drop it into a bureau drawer. But Bob would notice she was not wearing it and might fly into a rage. She was now convinced she was dealing with a man who, whatever the reason, was momentarily deranged.

Bob greeted her smilingly when she opened the door. "Let's go," he said. "The car's parked around a turn of the drive; I didn't want to get too near the house."

They were just inside the front door when the bell rang. It rang insistently three times, and then there were several knocks while a loud voice shouted:

"Open in the name of the law! Police!"

The lights were not on in the lower hall or on the porch. But the light from upstairs shone down. Anne looked toward Bob, or rather, where he had been a second before. He was no longer there or anywhere in sight. Her overnight case stood in the middle of the rug where he had dropped it.

Again the doorbell rang, and Anne collected herself enough to open it and snap on the lights. Immediately two state troopers came in, closely followed by Brad.

"We've brought the boy back." The first officer reached behind the other one and pulled Butch forward.

"Butch!" exclaimed Anne. "Where have you been? I didn't know you were out!"

"I saw a robbery," said Butch importantly. "The robber tied up the service station man and made him lie on the floor, just like on TV. Then he took a lot of money out of the cash register. I saw him. I was looking through the window."

"Butch, you shouldn't make up stories like that. What were you doing, anyway, down in the village at night all by yourself?"

"I was looking for Uncle Bob," the boy explained.

"His story is true," said one of the officers. "The gas station was robbed tonight. Luckily the attendant wasn't hurt, but the robber escaped."

"He had a handkerchief tied around his face, all but the eyes," Butch elaborated. "But I knew him anyway. It was Uncle Bob."

"You shouldn't say such things," said Anne, horrified.

"I got into the act," said Brad, "when I saw Butch running down the street. I didn't believe his story at first, but I called the troopers anyway. Of course the robber may not have been Bob Roe; he should have more sense than to stick up a station near Glenbrook."

"But why would he rob a gas station?" asked Anne.

Brad looked at Anne oddly as she raised her hand to push back a strand of hair which had fallen across her forehead. She knew he had caught the flash of the diamond and topaz ring. "For get-away money," he said. "I see he didn't have time to pawn the ring."

Jim and Mary Stone, awakened by the noise, joined the group in the hall. Confused explanations followed, and it was some minutes before Mary, after unraveling the main facts, took Butch firmly by the arm and marched him upstairs.

Jim Stone thanked the troopers, offered them a drink which they refused, and extracted what further details he could about the night's events. After they left, he bolted the front door after them.

"I'll just see the rest of the doors and

the windows are locked downstairs," he said. "No telling if the robber will take a notion to hide here. They don't really think it was Bob Roe do they?"

"I don't know," said Anne uncertainly.

Alone in the hall with Anne, Brad looked at her and then glanced toward the overnight case. "Bob Roe was here, wasn't he? Were you going away with him?"

"Yes, he broke into the house and came up to my room. I'm sure he had gone out of his mind. He ordered me to get up and get dressed and packed. He gave me the ring. He told me to pack an overnight case, and said we would go to Boston and catch a plane for Mexico. I was hoping I could get help somehow, somewhere, before I got on the plane."

"Had he cut the telephone wires?"

"I don't know. I didn't get a chance to phone . . ."

There were three staccato reports from not too far away. "Do you think that was a big truck backfiring?" she asked.

"Sounded like gunfire to me," said Brad shortly. "I'd better see what's going on. Lock the door after me." He was gone at once.

Anne locked the door, picked up her overnight case and went up to her room. She sat shivering on the bed for a while and finally tried the phone. It was dead. She forced herself to get into bed, but she slept only fitfully and was wide awake when the first ribbons of dawn streaked the sky with fragile pink.

After she had dressed and gone downstairs, she found the kitchen empty, but she made herself a cup of instant coffee and took it out to the English garden. She sat sipping it as she watched the sun's gold rim edging upward above the still dark mountains.

She didn't know until she heard it that she had been waiting for the sound of Brad's car. He came and sank into a chair beside her. He looked tired, and rubbed a hand wearily across his forehead.

"I tried to call you when I found out," he said after a second, "but your line was dead." Anne nodded. "The troopers caught up with Roe; it was gunfire we heard. They shot at the tires, and the car crashed. He was dead when I got there; the money from the gas station robbery was on him."

"Poor man!" Anne exclaimed. "Such a wasted life."

"You can say that again," Brad said, and got up. "Well, anyhow, it's all over now. Have you decided what you're going to do?"

"Yes," Anne replied. "I thought it through yesterday. I'll set up the rest home here with the medical advisory board. It will be difficult, I imagine, and there will be many problems. But maybe problems are what I need; I have to keep busy."

"And Steve?"

Anne shook her head. "It would

never work, Brad. I know that now. I don't love Steve; I have never loved him, really. And I don't now why. He's a wonderful man and a fine surgeon."

Brad sat down again, and it seemed to Anne he looked less tired. "Then you're giving up all thought of marriage for the immediate future?"

Anne spread her hands in a helpless gesture. "What else can I do? As you said yesterday, no man likes to be tied down to one place."

"There is one solution to your problem." Anne looked questioning. "You could marry the man next door!"

"I don't understand," Anne faltered.

Brad rose and came over to her chair. "I guess I'm doing it backward. I should have asked first: will you marry me?"

"And I should ask you first: do you love me?" Anne asked breathlessly.

Brad leaned over and pulled her to her feet, then crushed her in his arms. "Actions speak louder than words. Now

I have two questions: Do you? Will you?"

"Yes," Anne whispered. "Yes to both questions. Double yes!"

He picked her up in his arms and carried her to the house and across the threshold.

"Now," he said as he set her down, "you're in your dream home. Here at The Queen's Grant, together, we'll make your dreams of helping others come true."

THE END

WITH SOMEBODY ELSE
Theresa Charles

Rosamond sets off for Cornwall with Hugo to meet his family, blissfully unaware of the shocks in store for her.

A SUMMER FOR STRANGERS
Claire Hamilton

Because she had lost her job, her flat and she had no money, Tabitha agreed to pose as Adam's future wife although she believed the scheme to be deceitful and cruel.

VILLA OF SINGING WATER
Angela Petron

The disquieting incidents that occurred at the Vatican and the Colosseum did not trouble Jan at first, but then they became increasingly unpleasant and alarming.

DOCTOR NAPIER'S NURSE
Pauline Ash

When cousins Midge and Derry are entered as probationer nurses on the same day but at different hospitals they agree to exchange identities.

A GIRL LIKE JULIE
Louise Ellis

Caroline absolutely adored Hugh Barrington, but then Julie Crane came into their lives. Julie was the kind of girl who attracts men without even trying.

COUNTRY DOCTOR
Paula Lindsay

When Evan Richmond bought a practice in a remote country village he did not realise that a casual encounter would lead to the loss of his heart.

ENCORE
Helga Moray

Craig and Janet realise that their true happiness lies with each other, but it is only under traumatic circumstances that they can be reunited.

NICOLETTE
Ivy Preston

When Grant Alston came back into her life, Nicolette was faced with a dilemma. Should she follow the path of duty or the path of love?

THE GOLDEN PUMA
Margaret Way

Catherine's time was spent looking after her father's Queensland farm. But what life was there without David, who wasn't interested in her?

HOSPITAL BY THE LAKE
Anne Durham

Nurse Marguerite Ingleby was always ready to become personally involved with her patients, to the despair of Brian Field, the Senior Surgical Registrar, who loved her.

VALLEY OF CONFLICT
David Farrell

Isolated in a hostel in the French Alps, Ann Russell sees her fiancé being seduced by a young girl. Then comes the avalanche that imperils their lives.

NURSE'S CHOICE
Peggy Gaddis

A proposal of marriage from the incredibly handsome and wealthy Reagan was enough to upset any girl — and Brooke Martin was no exception.

A DANGEROUS MAN
Anne Goring

Photographer Polly Burton was on safari in Mombasa when she met enigmatic Leon Hammond. But unpredictability was the name of the game where Leon was concerned.

PRECIOUS INHERITANCE
Joan Moules

Karen's new life working for an authoress took her from Sussex to a foreign airstrip and a kidnapping; to a real life adventure as gripping as any in the books she typed.

VISION OF LOVE
Grace Richmond

When Kathy takes over the rundown country kennels she finds Alec Stinton, a local vet, very helpful. But their friendship arouses bitter jealousy and a tragedy seems inevitable.

CRUSADING NURSE
Jane Converse

It was handsome Dr. Corbett who opened Nurse Susan Leighton's eyes and who set her off on a lonely crusade against some powerful enemies and a shattering struggle against the man she loved.

WILD ENCHANTMENT
Christina Green

Rowan's agreeable new boss had a dream of creating a famous perfume using her precious Silverstar, but Rowan's plans were very different.

DESERT ROMANCE
Irene Ord

Sally agrees to take her sister Pam's place as La Chartreuse the dancer, but she finds out there is more to it than dyeing her hair red and looking like her sister.

HEART OF ICE
Marie Sidney

How was January to know that not only would the warmth of the Swiss people thaw out her frozen heart, but that she too would play her part in helping someone to live again?

LUCKY IN LOVE
Margaret Wood

Companion-secretary to wealthy gambler Laura Duxford, who lived in Monaco, seemed to Melanie a fabulous job. Especially as Melanie had already lost her heart to Laura's son, Julian.

NURSE TO PRINCESS JASMINE
Lilian Woodward

Nick's surgeon brother, Tom, performs an operation on an Arabian princess, and she invites Tom, Nick and his fiancé to Omander, where a web of deceit and intrigue closes about them.

THE WAYWARD HEART
Eileen Barry

Disaster-prone Katherine's nickname was "Kate Calamity", but her boss went too far with an outrageous proposal, which because of her latest disaster, she could not refuse.

FOUR WEEKS IN WINTER
Jane Donnelly

Tessa wasn't looking forward to meeting Paul Mellor again — she had made a fool of herself over him once before. But was Orme Jared's solution to her problem likely to be the right one?

SURGERY BY THE SEA
Sheila Douglas

Medical student Meg hadn't really wanted to go and work with a G.P. on the Welsh coast although the job had its compensations. But Owen Roberts was certainly not one of them!

HEAVEN IS HIGH
Anne Hampson

The new heir to the Manor of Marbeck had been found. But it was rather unfortunate that when he arrived unexpectedly he found an uninvited guest, complete with stetson and high boots.

LOVE WILL COME
Sarah Devon

June Baker's boss was not really her idea of her ideal man, but when she went from third typist to boss's secretary overnight she began to change her mind.

ESCAPE TO ROMANCE
Kay Winchester

Oliver and Jean first met on Swale Island. They were both trying to begin their lives afresh, but neither had bargained for complications from the past.

CASTLE IN THE SUN
Cora Mayne

Emma's invalid sister, Kym, needed a warm climate, and Emma jumped at the chance of a job on a Mediterranean island. But Emma soon finds that intrigues and hazards lurk on the sunlit isle.

BEWARE OF LOVE
Kay Winchester

Carol Brampton resumes her nursing career when her family is killed in a car accident. With Dr. Patrick Farrell she begins to pick up the pieces of her life, but is bitterly hurt when insinuations are made about her to Patrick.

DARLING REBEL
Sarah Devon

When Jason Farradale's secretary met with an accident, her glamorous stand-in was quite unable to deal with one problem in particular.